CW01661084

'What can I do for you, mister?'

Kane drew his revolver slowly from his holster. 'I wondered if you'd take a look at this, Mr Kells.'

The man looked startled. 'Kells?' he said, trying to force a laugh. He pointed towards the door. 'The name's Howard, mister.'

Kane still held the revolver in his hand. 'Your name is Kells and you're from Georgia,' he said slowly. 'Two years ago you robbed the Vicksburg lines of a great deal of cash, getting away with forty thousand dollars. You're worth four thousand . . . dead or alive.'

Kane cocked the hammer of his gun.

'And I'm claiming it!'

KILLING FOR THE LAW

Also by Louis Masterson

WITHOUT MERCY
THE CLAW OF THE DRAGON
THE STAR AND THE GUN
BACKED BY THE LAW
A RANGER'S HONOUR
MARSHAL AND MURDERER
PISTOLERO
THE MONSTER FROM YUMA
THE DEVIL'S MARSHAL
GUNSMAN'S INHERITANCE
REVENGE
STORM OVER SONORA
THE LAW OF THE JUNGLE
NO TEARS FOR MORGAN KANE
BETWEEN LIFE AND DEATH
RETURN TO ACTION
RIO GRANDE
BRAVADO
THE GALLOWS EXPRESS
RANSOM

and published by Corgi Books

Louis Masterson

Killing for The Law

CORGI BOOKS
A DIVISION OF TRANSWORLD PUBLISHERS LTD
A NATIONAL GENERAL COMPANY

KILLING FOR THE LAW

A CORGI BOOK 0 552 09287 8

First publication in Great Britain

PRINTING HISTORY
Corgi edition published 1973

Copyright © 1973 by Bladkompaniet A/S,
Storgaten 31, Oslo 1, Norway

Translated from the Norwegian by Phil Newth

This book is set in Intertype Plantin

Corgi Books are published by Transworld Publishers Ltd.,
Cavendish House, 57–59 Uxbridge Road,
Ealing, London W.5.
Made and printed in Great Britain by
Hunt Barnard Printing Ltd., Aylesbury, Bucks.

NOTE: The Australian price appearing on the back cover is the recommended retail price.

Killing for The Law

Chapter 1

A Winchester rifle, calibre 44/70, is an accurate, long-range weapon. The velocity of the bullet from the barrel is high, over three hundred yards per second, and the weight of the projectile plus the force of the gas pressure from the charge gives the weapon an unusual power.

This is what Ben Thompson had reckoned on as he lay up on the ridge waiting for the rider who within an hour or two would pass beneath him, roughly four hundred yards behind him. Thompson also had a smaller rifle, a short carbine, of smaller calibre. This weapon was lighter and handier than the heavy Winchester but its precision and range was far inferior to that of the larger rifle. The carbine was all right for saddle use, quick firing at close quarters and fast loading. It was a weapon well suited to, for example, Indian wars. But there had been no Indian uprising in Texas since the end of the seventies, so the man must have had other things in mind when he decided to use two different types of rifle.

In addition to the two rifles, the man carried a .45 Colt with a bone handle. If one looked closer one would see six notches that had been filed into the one butt plate. He had placed a brown and ochre coloured Navajo blanket under him. Within range lay four extra bullets for the Winchester, a roll of chewing tobacco, a hunting knife and a piece of dried venison, packed in a piece of fat-covered hide. Hidden behind him in the bushes stood a large, grey horse and two heavy saddle bags, a blanket roll and other camping equipment was leaning against a rock. The equipment was well used, simple and practical.

He lay very still, his legs apart and elbows on the ground. His hat was pulled well down over his eyes to protect them from the evening sun that would be almost facing him soon. He would rather have had the sun on his back but the terrain on the other side of the valley didn't offer enough cover or target area.

He lay there – listening to the noises brought on the wind – and had no eyes for the beauty of the landscape around him; the grass down at the bottom of the valley, the flowers and bushes along the small river and the wispy clouds that drifted slowly eastwards in the evening breeze. Ben Thompson was no ordinary traveller, or hunter, adventurer or gold miner.

He was a professional murderer.

A bounty hunter.

He was thirty-three years old and had been a bounty hunter since he was twenty-seven. The men he had hunted were not ordinary men either. Ordinary men didn't have prices on their heads. There had been some that even Thompson shuddered to think of. They had been as wary as animals, with animal instincts and senses. Pure luck had saved him three times when he had underestimated the man he was hunting and discovered that *he* – Thompson – was the hunted. But he had made it and lived long enough to learn from his experience. He had, after a while, developed a certain instinct, to put himself in the place of the hunted man, think like him, react like him, know his movements beforehand. He took all measures and left nothing to luck. That's why he had done all right for himself – earning roughly fifteen thousand dollars a year, money which he saved a little of, some he used in the gambling houses and brothels in the towns up north – Wichita, Kansas City and St Louis.

There was nothing about Thompson's appearance that revealed his profession. There was nothing blood-thirsty, sadistic or evil about the brown, narrow face. There was nothing weak about his eyes, no revealing mouth lines. He may have been a cattle drover, coach driver or miner.

But he was a bounty hunter.

His horse snorted quietly.

Thompson wasn't startled, didn't leap up – because he knew that the horse would hear the sounds from the valley floor before he would. Perhaps his eyes narrowed slightly and maybe his hands around the rifle gripped the rifle tighter – that was all.

A few minutes later he heard it; sounds of shod hooves against the stones along the river. A smile flickered in the corners of Thompson's mouth. The man down there had discovered that he was being chased. To hide his tracks he had either ridden in the river itself or on the stony bank. The man was not very experienced, Thompson thought, he himself would never have ridden into such a narrow valley – river or no river. On the other hand, he thought, the man down there couldn't know that Thompson had ridden past him already the day before and had seen the natural route he would follow.

As the sounds grew louder he began to judge the light and wind. Then he caught sight of the rider at the bend of the river. It was just a slow, dark speck against the green but after a while he could make out the hat, the horse's legs and the blanket roll, behind the saddle. There was still a matter of minutes before the rider was level with him, and Thompson used the time to study the animal's rhythm of movement. It would be a shot at about three hundred yards, and the least movement that wasn't calculated beforehand would mean a miss and weeks of hunting before he came into range again.

The rider down there stopped his horse. Thompson saw that he stood in the stirrups and stared at the river up the valley and the slopes on each side. The horse was uneasy, not liking the slippery, round stones on the river bank.

Come on, Jim, Thompson thought, come nearer . . . nothing to be scared of. Just ride on a little . . .

Jimmy Fresno spurred his horse and trotted along the river bank. Thompson could almost *see* the man's suspicion, the thoughts of ambush. . . . But he had no reason to believe that Thompson had ridden past him, even less reason to think that he was waiting in *this* valley. But he kept his rifle across his knees as he rode – nearer and nearer the two pines that Thompson had sorted out as the border.

When Fresno was fifty yards from the pines, Thompson cocked the Winchester and placed his cheek against the butt. The wind against his cheek was almost unnoticeable. He could ignore the pressure of wind. The light came in from the left so he had to take into consideration the tiny ray of light on the sight. The sight was on four hundred yards – a little too high, so Thompson lowered the sights slightly.

Fresno rode into the shade of the pines.

Thompson's right finger lay around the trigger. He breathed deeply a couple of times and as his eye found the figure just above the sight, he exhaled slowly.

The shot roared down the valley. As soon as the heavy recoil had thumped his shoulder Thompson reloaded, driving another bullet up the spout. His sighting-eye hadn't left Jimmy Fresno for a second – if it was going to be necessary with another shot.

But it wasn't. The figure down there was blown half out of the saddle and the horse leapt forward in terror. Fresno fell down on the far side from Thompson and was dragged three yards or so before lying still with one leg out in the river.

Thompson still kept the sight on him for some seconds, then he lowered the hammer, got up and began to walk down the slope with the rifle at the ready. Fresno's horse had ridden a hundred yards farther up. It stood and stared at him. It was a good horse, Thompson thought, surely worth a hundred dollars up north.

He approached Fresno carefully, making sure he came up on Fresno's left side – the opposite side of his revolver hand, but Fresno lay just as still. Thompson turned him over with his foot, knelt down and checked the bullet wound. Fresno's face and eyes, even in death, had an expression of petrified surprise. A small graze in the forehead sent a dark trickle of blood down to the temple.

It was a tiny hole, just a nick where the bullet had torn the skin in a star-shape, where the bullet had gone in, just under the shoulder. The bullet had passed straight through the body and out just by the left chest muscle. Here there was a terrible hole.

Thompson got up and rolled a cigarette. He listened a while before he lit it. There was pride and joy in his eyes. It had been a fantastic shot.

A three thousand dollar shot.

Amarillo lies in the north-west part of Texas, between the Canadian and Big Prairie rivers. Already in the early sixties this town – a cattle town – was known for its violence and lawlessness. Cattle drovers and their herds brought with them, from the south, a number of adventurers, outlaws, gunmen and, of course, the usual drovers who sweated for their forty dollars a month plus grub.

In 1878 the infamous Shanghai Pearce passed the town and one of his boys was put in jail by a town marshal, Pickering, because he shot a woman. The man swore that it was a pure accident, and Shanghai Pearce backed his statement. He fumbled with a roll of bills and wanted to settle the matter the easy way. Unfortunately, Pickering took his job seriously and told Pearce to get the hell out of the town. The woman-killer was put in the town's jail and Pearce and his bunch left Amarillo. Pickering breathed a sigh of relief and started to plan a trial.

That night Shanghai Pearce returned – and he came like a tornado. Twenty riders with lassoes and buffalo ropes just tore down the old building into bits and pieces. Marshal Pickering hadn't even time to get his clothes on – just grabbed the first and best weapon he could – a double-barrelled shotgun – and rushed out in his underclothes. What happened then is uncertain. But when Shanghai Pearce rode out again, Pickering lay full of holes in the street and the woman killer had disappeared with his buddies.

The town council came together, chose a new marshal and built a new prison – of stone. The sheriff's office was placed in one wing, and the eight iron-barred cells were entered from the sheriff's office. Pickering's son – the twenty-year-old Ed – was voted new town marshal and soon life resumed its normal pace. At first the new prison awoke a lot of interest and the inhabitants of the town were very proud of it – maybe because it was a joint enterprise and a symbol of law and order in town.

When Ben Thompson rode into town ten years after Shanghai Pearce, Ed Pickering was a man of almost thirty, a dark, lean man with grey streaks at the temples. The star on his vest told that he was now a district sheriff and had three full-time deputies working for him, and five others that were available for special occasions.

That summer day in 1888 it was hot and stifling in the office, and Pickering sat in shirt sleeves and stared out of the window down the street. There was little traffic in the street. It was much too quiet really. Not until late summer – when the herd went north from the enormous cattle areas in mid-Texas –

would Amarillo spring to life. Then the corrals around the railway station would be packed with huge, bellowing Longhorns which would be shipped west to Wichita and Kansas City, which was the centre for cattle dealing in the mid-West.

Pickering thought of this as a cigar burned in the ash tray beside him. Ever since that day ten years before when the men had come back with his father his life had been one long, nerve-racking wait. Waiting for the day when gangs of wild cowpokes came yelling and shooting into town. Ed Pickering despised them. He had killed four cow drovers in cold blood in the last few years, drunken boys who had shot too haphazardly with their shooting irons. The first year he wore a star he banned the cowpokes from carrying arms inside the town's limits. It took him months of struggle while he had men sitting in his cells while their mates headed east again. Some ended in the hospital, some on Boot Hill – the town's wind-swept, naked graveyard. Finally the ban was respected and Ed Pickering's name followed every cattle route in all directions. Before he was twenty-four he was known as one of the 'greats' – in company with Virgil, Morgan and Wyatt Earp, James Hickock, Bat Masterson, and Johnny Hayes. But, like these men, Ed Pickering had to pay for the honour. He knew, without doubt, that sooner or later, one of the cowdrovers would start shooting at him – and get him. Sooner or later there would be one among them who drew faster than he did. There was always one who was faster. And the more he used his iron, the quicker he would stumble across the man.

Pickering crushed the smoking cigar butt and sighed. He was bored. But he still hated the thought of August. That's when they arrived. Till then he would just have to wait. Wake at night, soaked in sweat, wondering if it was his last autumn.

He caught sight of the rider down the street. A pack-horse with a bundle across the saddle trudged behind. Pickering leaned forward and rubbed some of the dust off the window pane. He could see that it was a person – a man – who lay over the saddle. The head dangled grotesquely to and fro. Pickering was furious. The damned fool – he could at least have rolled the body in a blanket or piece of canvas. People began to notice the macabre procession. A couple of boys ran beside the packhorse. A couple of men followed along the pavement. Pickering saw them trying to converse with the rider, but the stranger looked neither to right or left.

Pickering leaned back in the chair and swung it to face the door. His hand slipped on to his revolver under the table. On the wall to the left of the door half a dozen faces stared at him from wanted posters. He wondered which one of them he could tear down.

Somebody knocked on the door and a tall, thin man entered with his hat in his hand. It wasn't done with respect or politeness – he'd just knocked the dust off his clothes with it.

'Sheriff,' the stranger said, 'this is Jimmy Fresno.' He went over to the wall, tore down one of the wanted posters and lay it on the table in front of Pickering. Fresno's young, handsome face stared up at them.

'And who are you?' Pickering asked mildly. The disgust he felt for bounty hunters was still only showing in his eyes.

'The name is Thompson. Ben Thompson. I'm in a hurry, so I hope you can get a telegram sent off as fast as possible. Maybe the price has gone up.'

'Nope,' Pickering answered. 'It's still at three thousand.'

'Okay. Wanna take a look at him?'

'Sure.'

Pickering frowned when he saw the crowd of curious people gathered round the corpse. He sneered, 'Why in hell didn't you wrap him in something?'

'Didn't want any bloodstains on my blankets.'

'Next time you ride in here, Thompson, with a dead man, I'd advise you to wrap him in something. Get it?'

Something in Pickering's voice warned Thompson to tread carefully now.

'All right, Sheriff.'

Pickering only needed to glance at the dirty face. They went back to the office. Pickering took out a paper and pencil and wrote a short explanation which Thompson signed.

'I'll send the telegram now,' Pickering said. 'Staying here in town, meanwhile?'

'Yeah . . . at the hotel.'

'All right. You'll hear from me in a couple of hours.'

'Thanks, Sheriff.' Thompson's eyes showed his joy. 'Gotta

admit us bloodhounds sure save you lawmen a lotta saddle sores!'

Pickering looked him in the eye. 'Far as I'm concerned you can ride all the way to hell, you damned vulture!'

Thompson chuckled, put his hat on and led his horse across to the hotel.

Pickering walked down to the telegraph office. He sent the telegram to the district sheriff in Dallas and was told the answer would arrive in an hour's time. He nodded, put on his hat and went back to his office. That was the fourth that year. The first three were worth five hundred each. Easily earned cash, he thought, lighting a cigar. He wondered how these bounty hunters slept at night. Then he reconsidered the thought. They slept well, okay. It was he himself who. . . . He suddenly got up and went over to the window. Thompson's horse was tied outside the hotel. Pickering puffed at his cigar.

Ben Thompson sat in the bar in the hotel with a bottle of whisky in front of him. He was tired yet satisfied. In a couple of hours a telegram would arrive with authority for him to draw the money from the bank. And then . . . ? A good drink, a woman or two – then another trip north. Thompson raised his glass to himself.

Three men walked casually across the floor to him and stopped by his table. Thompson looked up at them. They stared back. The oldest of them – a squarely-built man in his forties – smiled and said:

'You the one that brought in Jimmy Fresno?'

'Yeah. What about it?'

'We've been on his tail for seven weeks.'

Thompson smiled. 'That's life, boys. Better luck next time.'

'We look at it this way – he was ours, Thompson.'

'I didn't notice any name-plate on him.'

'Can we sit down?'

Thompson nodded, but moved the bottle first. The three men exchanged looks. There was nothing extraordinary about them, a fact that put Thompson on his guard.

'My name's Caine,' the grey-haired man said. 'These are my partners Conway and Waldron.'

'Ben Thompson.'

'We've heard about you,' Caine said. 'Don't you usually

operate out east?'

'Yeah, but business ain't so hot out there right now.'

'You thinking of . . . er . . . doing business here in Texas a while, Thompson?'

Thompson's eyes narrowed. 'What's it with you?'

Caine smiled. 'This has sorta been our district,' he said. 'We don't like competition. A lotta hunters means less game.'

'I'll do okay for myself,' Thompson answered.

Caine and his men exchanged looks again. 'Hope you don't mind me saying that you young 'uns are too quick on the trigger,' he went on. 'Take Jimmy Fresno. The price was three thousand. In two or three months he would have been worth five thousand. Get what I mean? We had Frenso grazing, Thompson – we were fattening him, I could say.'

'I ain't greedy,' Thompson said. 'Three thousand dollars is a lotta green.'

Caine's eyes were two piercing specks. 'All right,' he said. 'I'll say it fast and clear. We don't want you around here, Thompson. This is our district. We're organised. But as you're good at it and I like your face I'll offer you a deal. Come in with us. You can make a lotta cash and I mean a *lot*. Not small fry like Jimmy Fresno.'

Thompson emptied his glass and put it down.

'Answer is no. I like being a loner.'

'Okay.' The men got up. Caine twirled his hat through his fingers. He looked at Thompson. 'It's a shame,' he mumbled. 'Damn shame.' He turned and the other two followed him out.

Thompson sat a while thinking. He knew that the smartest thing would be to get out of Amarillo soon. There were three of them. Okay, he thought, Texas is big enough anyway.

He went over to the sheriff's office later, got the answer he wanted from Ed Pickering and drew the money out of the Amarillo Trust Bank. He shoved the bills into his money belt, saddled his horse and left town.

Half an hour later Caine and his boys left town too, in the same direction. Four hours later a rifle shot roared in a valley east of Amarillo.

Ben Thompson had – the irony of fate – been shot down by a sneak-murderer's bullet.

Chapter 2

U.S. marshal Ed Zachary turned a broad back towards the dusty window and looked at the man behind the writing desk.

'If you want my opinion it's a typical "Kane" job,' he said.

Shane leaned back in the huge chair and studied the handsome marshal. Zachary was perhaps the only man in Fort Leavenworth who really knew Morgan Kane, or at least knew him better than anyone – if *anyone* knew him at all. It was he who had persuaded Kane to join the corps of marshals after handing in his star as a Texas ranger – which Kane had done under harrowing circumstances. But Shane didn't know if Zachary *liked* Kane. It was his own uncertainty that made him ask:

'What do you really think of Kane, Ed?' Shane knew that he couldn't demand an answer. Zachary was a hard, simple man with a personal sense of justice and right. What he really thought of the much more complicated character who was Morgan Kane couldn't, perhaps, be put into words.

Zachary turned towards the window again. The sun turned the dust to an orange shade. He said slowly, 'I'm durned if I know.'

Shane considered it for a while. 'You've worked with him often enough. What's he like?' It was a clumsy, groping question but Shane couldn't phrase it in any other way. When Kane was away Shane had to fill the empty gap that his absence had made in the corps. Because Kane had left a gaping hole in Fort Leavenworth, and they hadn't found anybody who could fill it. He was back again now and had assignment number three to face. Shane had realised that the same thing could happen again if Kane wasn't handled in the right way. His wife's death had made a sadist of him, and with his ability with a gun it had made him a much more dangerous man than Shane had ever reckoned on. But now – now it had become more a thing of the past – Shane could follow Kane's revenge and then the months he had spent in an alcoholic daze by the Rio Grande, until a spark had set light to the fuse in him and started Kane once again on the rampage. Kane was no young man when he married. The shock of losing his wife, his lifeline, was a catastrophe for him. Shane knew that there would always be a danger that Kane would go fighting crazy again. He'd like to know Kane so well that he could recognise the signs of an approaching fit. Shane knew that if his superiors in the government found out just how changed Kane was, he would get a severe reprimand, maybe lose his job and Kane would definitely get kicked out. Kane was as explosive as a smoking bomb, a bomb wearing a silver star. But he was also the most able marshal in Fort Leavenworth and Shane depended on him. A glance at the papers on his desk proved it. They had nobody except Kane who *could*, possibly, solve this case.

Shane had put him on to the smuggling case in Cuba when he returned and Kane had smashed the gang completely – almost losing his life in the attempt. They had dragged him out of the smoking mausoleum a few seconds before the building collapsed on him.

Kane had been effective and able, seemingly his old self again. But Shane had heard him mumbling wildly in his hospital bed and knew that Kane was now balancing on rock bottom.

'What's he like?' he had asked.

'He's hard,' Zachary said. 'I've never seen such a tough nut as Kane. He's stood up to more than any other person I know. But he's beginning to show cracks. He's no machine. He's weak about women; women and liquor are his failings. I've often wondered if somewhere deep inside he's . . . well . . . got any feelings. But his childhood and youth wouldn't have helped his feelings at all. He was born in a wagon on the Santa-Fe trail and blood and death were the first impressions he had of life. He's a result of life on the border. The point is – Kane is *still* alive and is still around to make others wonder about it. All the others are dead . . . Kells, Bonney, Bland, Duane . . . all the others are dead. Kane's still alive.'

Zachary looked at Shane, who stared at him in surprise.

'But I just don't *know* him,' he added.

Shane looked at the glow of his cigar. Zachary was right, Kane belonged to the bloody, wild, devil-may-care generation who, for good and bad, had changed the border regions.

The former generation.

'All right,' he said. 'I'll put Kane on the job.'

'Kane'll fix it,' Zachary answered.

It was suddenly quiet in the large, warm office. Shane stared out at the shimmering, white sunshine. That's how the sun was shining out there across the white salt plains by the Rio Grande. What had happened out there by the border? What had happened before the ranger had sent that sensational telegram?

'Ask him to step in,' Shane said.

Zachary disappeared.

Shane was almost half way through the pile of papers when the door was knocked.

Kane entered and nodded to Shane. Zachary shut the door behind him and didn't sit down.

'Sit down, boys,' Shane said. He looked at the lean, dark man in front of him.

'I've got a job for you, Morgan.'

Kane didn't answer. His face was without expression. The grey, almost colourless eyes were fastened on Shane. His long, brown fingers were across his knees. He looked competent, relaxed. Shane suddenly felt relieved.

'Feel okay?' he added, briefly.

'Yes.'

'Good. Zachary's been in Amarillo. We've lost a man down there. Shot in the back down a backstreet. The sheriff in town – Pickering – hasn't found the murderer.'

Kane glanced at Zachary. The older marshal said, 'I had another job. Just dropped in.'

Shane's eyes narrowed. It was the first time he'd noticed anything like this between the two men. He said sharply, 'Our man – Vincent – was investigating a case we've been chewing on for some time – bounty hunting.

Kane straightened almost unnoticeably in the chair. Shane noticed it.

'We don't know what Vincent found or why he was killed. We know nothing. You've got to take over the case and you may just as well start in Amarillo. Ed Pickering is the sheriff there, a good man. Talk with him.'

Kane rolled a cigarette casually. The thin leather band holding the long and ring finger together didn't seem to bother him at all.

'Up to now the state has paid out over thirty thousand dollars in reward money,' Shane said. 'We believe that this is a case of *organised* bounty hunting. It's got to stop.'

'Why not start with the rewards?' Kane added dryly.

Shane smiled slightly. 'The law allows for rewards, Morgan. There is no federal law against that. Each county or district has a free hand. But the governor's office keeps a close watch on these rewards, and there is proof of a few hundred per cent rise in them recently. In a way I understand those dealing out the rewards. It's one way to put a stop to criminal activity. Last year in Kansas state there was about five thousand dollars paid out in rewards to bounty hunters. Up to now this year the figure is almost a hundred and thirty thousand for Texas, Kansas, New Mexico and Arizona. The average for these states is between five and seven thousand a year. The authorities want this rise looked into and stopped.'

'Can't the authorities do anything?'

'Of course. But these rewards are usually promised by the *towns,* and one doesn't want to get involved in local town politics. This increase points to an organised gang and covers a few states. The job is really ours and belongs here. I've got a pile of reports from county sheriffs who have paid out rewards for these killings. It's usually the same "hunters" that turn up but we don't have any of their names in the archives so they must be false names.'

'Let's get this straight,' Kane said. 'The rewards are promised. Anyone can put away the victim and collect the reward. There's nothing illegal about that.'

'Correct. But the increase is *not* due to a sudden increase in criminal or crime statistics,' Shane pointed out. 'It just looks as if this gang – if they are a gang – looks like really cleaning up on this thing. And *bigger* rewards are offered and they increase each month. It's a very strange coincidence. The governor thinks so too. *I* certainly do.'

'All right,' Kane said impatiently. 'But I still repeat what I said – there's nothing illegal, directly illegal about this.'

Shane exchanged looks with Zachary. Here it comes, the eyes said.

'You're right,' Shane said casually. 'There's no order for arrest in black and white for these bounty hunters. That's your job, Morgan, to *prove* that there is something illegal about this affair. You have a free hand.'

Kane leaned back in his chair. A job that just seemed to hang in the air. He'd had jobs like this before. For a moment he thought of the men who wandered into town with their macabre bundles – men that killed for a handful of dollars.

'A free hand,' he repeated – like an echo from the past when he heard the Ranger boss Monroe give the same orders.

'We have nothing else to work on,' Shane said. 'Start with Ed Pickering. He . . . '

'I know Pickering,' Kane said.

Shane was amazed. 'Oh?'

'I got into a fix once for gunning down a guy at the card table. Self defence.' Kane made a grimace when he said it. 'Pickering kicked me out of town.'

'He bears no grudges,' Shane said.

'Wouldn't have made any odds, either way . . . sir,' Kane added. His colourless eyes were suddenly cold and piercing.

'All right,' Shane said. 'You head for Amarillo tomorrow.'

Kane rose. He glanced at Zachary then walked towards the door. Shane nodded to Zachary who followed Kane. They walked side by side down the long corridor. The echo of their boots thundered between the stone walls.

'Beer, Morgan?'

'All right.'

They blew the foam off their glasses and looked around the mess. They nodded to half a dozen men. It was noticeable that nobody came over to their table to chat.

Kane looked at Zachary over his glass. 'Meet Ed Pickering?'

'Sure. Nice guy. Looks like his pa. He was killed by Shanghai Pearce in eighty-seven. You'll have no trouble with him.'

Kane drank deeply from the mug. His stomach knotted. The night was full of memories and fear and he fought to keep them at a distance.

He pushed the empty glass across the table. 'Another?'

'Yes, thanks.'

They sat there and chatted. There was no warmth or friendship between them. They weren't like that. They *had* to stand alone – completely. Hours passed. Men entered and left the mess, young and middle-aged. One thing in common which they all had was the way they held their right arm at their sides and the way they glanced to each side. They all carried a star in a leather wallet in their back pockets, but the *law* – their Colt .44 Police Special – they wore on their hips.

Kane suddenly wanted to get away from this nerve-wracking atmosphere. He sat drumming his fingers on the counter. Lack of action was getting him down. He suddenly felt a desperate need for alcohol. 'Think I'll take a nap,' he said, getting up. 'See you later, Ed.'

'Yeah,' Zachary said. He watched Kane's tall, lean figure disappear.

I wish I could just *talk* to him, he thought.

Chapter 3

Ed Pickering got up when Kane came into the sheriff's office. His face bore no expression when he offered his hand to Kane.

'Howdy, Kane. Long time no see.'

They shook hands.

'Sit down,' Pickering said calmly.

'Thanks,' Kane was relieved. It looked as if Pickering was going to be on his best behaviour. Great. That suited him fine.

'Vincent was buried yesterday. The town paid for the funeral.'

Kane just nodded.

'Here's the report and the information I've gathered.'

The sheriff went over to the window while Kane read through it. He was soon finished. Shane had already told him everything that was written there.

'No eye witnesses, Sheriff?' he asked.

'No. There never is in cases like this.' Kane noticed disdain in his voice but ignored it.

Pickering stared at him. 'This has something to do with those bounty hunters, right?'

Kane paused, not sure of how much Pickering knew or should know.

'Yeah,' he said. 'There's a bit too much of it recently.'

Pickering stared at him. 'A week ago a guy comes in here and gets three thousand for a bank robber from Dallas, Jimmy Fresno. A couple of days later he was found in a ditch a few miles from the county border. He called himself Ben Thompson. I think it was his real name – he was known farther eastaways for the same business.'

'How was he killed?'

'Rifle. In the back.'

Kane raised his eyebrows.

Pickering smiled. 'Sure, same calibre.'

'Was this Thompson alone?'

'He came alone here and rode out alone.'

Kane considered it. He looked at the sheriff. He decided to trust him suddenly. He had no choice. Shane had told him to operate as a private individual until there was proof that the bounty hunters had federal crimes hanging round their necks. And he'd need help – the law's help.

'If we assume that Thompson was a lone wolf who pushed his way on to this gang's territory then it *could* be the same finger on the trigger.'

'You mean that they want this district all to themselves? It ain't impossible – that is, if an organised gang of bounty hunters exist. You lot got any proof of it?'

'No. Anybody visit Thompson while he hung around town?'

'No.' Pickering glanced at Kane. 'Maybe you've got something there, Kane.'

'Maybe.' Kane got up. 'He stay at the hotel?'

'That's what he said. I had to get down to the telegraph office so I ain't sure.'

'I'll be dropping in again,' Kane said, over his shoulder.

'Do that,' the sheriff answered.

The hotel lobby was empty. A couple of dusty small palms stood withered in a pot. Kane could hear the sound of dishes being washed from the kitchen that lay backing on to the wall of the lobby. He hit the bell. A young boy appeared.

'You wantin' somethin', mister?'

Kane met the bright, blue eyes beneath the fringe of hair. 'Remember the guy that brought in a dead man last week?' he asked, as friendly as possible.

The boy nodded eagerly. 'You betcha, mister! It was real . . . grim.' It looked as if the boy thought his expression too manly. He rubbed his neck and went on, 'Well, he was kinda blue in the face. His head was hanging down, ya see,' he added.

'All right. Was that man in the hotel at all?'

'Can't rightly say, mister. I was off duty then. Didn't start until four. From eight till two I work at a stable jest down the street here and . . . '

'Okay,' Kane said, 'can you find out if he was here at all?' A silver dollar shone beside Kane's hand.

'You betcha, mister!' He dived out of the back door and Kane sat on a chest up against the wall, pushed his hat on to the back of his head and rolled a cigarette. A cutting female voice bellowed through the kitchen wall.

'She's callin' herself *Mrs* Dawson but I ain't too sure about that – her with eyes like a doggone bitch. Minnie says she's had a lotta men up in her room and not just once, mind ya, and that ol' bed shakes as if an ol' ram's a battering away in there, least that's what Minnie says.'

Another voice, husky with curiosity and enjoyable disgust, asked: 'Has she heard *that*?'

Kane smiled to himself.

'Jest *that*, yeah,' the first one answered, triumphantly.

The boy came dashing back and poured out the details to Kane.

'Mister Greaves was on watch, sir. He says he stayed in the bar. The barkeeper's called Solomon. He was workin' when that there bounty hunter came in. He'll remember him for sure, mister.'

'Thanks a lot.' Kane flipped a silver dollar over to him. 'Order a room for me at the same time, will you? The name is Kane.'

'Yessir, Mr Kane, sir. And thank you, sir. You can walk right through the dining-room into the bar.'

Kane nodded to the boy, walked through the almost empty dining-room and into the long, narrow, dark bar. A swarthy little man with hanging moustaches and long, greasy side whiskers was polishing glasses.

Kane sat at the bar. Through the glass he measured the distance to the nearest guests. They were well outside earshot.

'Mr Solomon?' Kane said, quietly.

'That's me, sir.' The man spoke broken English.

'Last week a man was here with a dead man.'

'In *here*, sir?'

'No, in town. He raised a bounty on him.' Kane realised that this Solomon wasn't as green as he was making out to be. He put a ten-dollar bill on the counter. The smile on Solomon's face disappeared. He now wore a business-like expression.

'That's right, sir. I served him myself.'

'Where did he sit?'

'Over by the long wall. Third table from the left.'

'Was he sitting alone?'

'All alone.'

Well, Kane thought, that was that. Twelve dollars out of the window.

'Until three men came over and talked to him,' Solomon said.

Kane looked at him.

'Know who the three were?'

'No, sir. Never set eyes on them before.'

'Did they talk long with him?'

'A few minutes. Ten, maybe fifteen. Maybe half an hour. I don't remember.'

'Did they sit at his table?'

'Not straight away.'

'You serve the three at the table?'

'No.'

'Were you near the table while they sat there?'

'Well . . . guess I was. Fetched the glasses, wiped the tables . . . You know . . . ' He made a gesture explaining his movements.

'All right,' Kane said, dryly. 'You hear what they talked about?'

'Oh . . . my memory's terrible. Almost as bad as my hearing.'

Kane placed another ten-dollar bill on the table. 'Use this for an ear check-up, Mr Solomon,' he said casually.

'I'll do just that, sir! Now, let's see . . . ' Solomon's squirrel-like face frowned in deep thought. 'I've got it!' he exclaimed, suddenly.

'Let's have it,' Kane said coldly.

'One of the three, the one who did all the talking, by the way, said something about "organisation". The bounty hunter said he liked working alone. That's all I heard, sir. Two things, sorry.'

I'll bet you are, you bastard, Kane thought. But by a stroke of luck these two bits were enough. The rest of the jig-saw he already had.

'Ain't much for twenty dollars, Solomon,' Kane said. 'But you ain't done yet. Describe the three as best you can. Details, things you found unusual. Think deeply and try to describe them, clothes, hats, boots, weapons – and their faces, height, weight . . . anything you remember.'

Solomon's face was contorted as if in pain. 'I remember him best, the talkative one, sir, he was the boss I guess. He gave me that impression. He was tall, almost as tall as you, sir, but bigger made . . . er . . . fatter, would be better. He had grey streaks in his hair and had light skin. Wore an ordinary dark suit and I think he had a black hat.'

'Guns?'

'I didn't see any, sir.'

'See his eyes?'

'No, sir. I saw him from the side. Wait a little! I think – ain't sure, mind you – his nose was busted. Had a strange shape, like a sabre – if you know what I mean?'

'Get it. Anything else?'

Solomon paused. 'No, sir.'

'All right. And the others?'

Solomon threw out his hands. 'The others, sir? They just *were* there. They kind of . . . well, didn't stand out. They said nothing, just sat there. They were two, what we call in bar-language, "No face".'

'I get it.' Kane pushed the bar stool away. 'Thanks, Mr Solomon. Don't forget to get your ears checked.'

'I won't, sir. Er . . . I mean forget to check 'em!'

Kane left the bar and walked out into the white sunshine. He felt the sweat on his back. He walked over the street into a café and ordered a beer. He sat in a cool corner and sat looking out at the street, drinking his beer. It was cold, pleasant. He ordered another. When he had finished the beer he wrote the information down on a piece of paper. He read it a few times then he picked out the most important parts and drafted a telegram. When he had finished it he paid and went down to the telegraph office. He sent the telegram to Fort Leavenworth and asked the telegraphist to bring the reply to the hotel. The telegraphist promised to do it.

The boy stood behind the counter.

'Number thirty-four on the second, Mr Kane. Will you sign here?'

Kane signed, took his key and started to walk away. Then he turned.

'I've got two saddle bags down in the stable. Could you fetch 'em and bring 'em up to my room?'

'Right away, Mr Kane.'

Kane flipped half a dollar to him and the boy disappeared like an arrow.

The room was stuffy and dark. He drew back the curtains and opened the window. The sun was on its way west. He opened his jacket, loosened his holster in his trouser waistline and threw it over on to the bed. He took off the thin linen shirt, washed himself with the luke-warm water in the jug and dressed again. There was a knock on the door and the boy came in with his saddle bags. Kane gave him five dollars and asked him to fetch a bottle of Old Grand-dad and a mug of cold water.

'*Cold* water, sir?'

Kane chuckled. 'Okay, *water*, then.'

When the bottle came Kane sat by the window and watched the sundown. It was like a spectacular play. The wind drove light clouds of dust from the dry plains, dust that turned to gold-dust in the rays of the dying sun. After a while it grew darker and the town came to life. He heard bursts of laughter from the street. A group of cowboys ran down the street whooping wildly. Payday, Kane reflected. He drank the whisky slowly. When he was sitting with his third glass a knock came on the door.

'Telegram, sir,' the boy said.

Kane flipped him another half-dollar. He opened the telegram and read it.

DESCRIPTION FITS A PETER CAINE STOP WANTED FOR MURDER AND ROBBERY WITH VIOLENCE IN EASTERN STATES STOP BEEN WITH TOM CONWAY AND JAMES WALDRON THE LAST FEW YEARS STOP BOTH WANTED FOR SIMILAR CRIMES STOP HAVE YOU ANYTHING ELSE YET STOP.

Kane filled his glass again and put his feet on the table. He wondered if he should show Pickering the telegram. No, not yet, not before he had something more concrete to build on and really needed help.

He discovered that he was slightly drunk and wondered if he should get really smashed out of his mind. He dropped the idea. Wasn't the right time really. Instead he stuck the holster in the top of his trousers and checked that the rubber loops were in place. He made sure the revolver was loaded, dropped it into the holster, put on his hat and jacket and locked the door.

It was deliciously cool in the street. He wandered the streets until he felt like a drink. He went into the town's biggest saloon and ordered a whisky at the bar. The place was full of cowboys who were drinking, playing cards and dancing. The rattle of silver dollars over at the Black-Jack table played on his nerves. Kane was a habitual gambler. He just loved the dense, sticky excited feeling around a table which was playing for high stakes. But he held himself in check. He knew he was in no condition to play carefully with three-quarters of a bottle of whisky inside him. He would be noticed and that wasn't good.

A gang of red-faced, sweating cowboys pushed their way towards the bar. They had just been dancing and laughed and joked with each other, arguing humorously about the girls. One of them bumped against Kane, spilling some of his drink. Kane moved to one side and said nothing. The cowboy misunderstood the movement. He said clearly: 'I was aimin' on saying sorry, mister – but I can't say I like the way you moved aside. Don't you like the smell o' horses? Maybe you prefer your own perfume?'

Kane didn't answer, just looked down into his glass.

'Cut it out, Will,' one of his friends said. 'Let's get a beer and get back to the girls.'

'Beer's okay, but I still want to know if this smarty here can stand the smell of horses.' His voice was thick and sneering and a glance at the red, bloated face told Kane that the man was looking for a fight.

He emptied his glass and put it down on the bar with a crash. A silver dollar rattled on the bar, then he turned and began to walk out.

'Hey you . . . !'

Kane whirled around. The cowboy's right fist grazed Kane's shoulder. Kane clenched his left and buried it into the soft part of the man's gut with all his might. Before the man had sunk to his knees Kane had disappeared in the crush of people.

He didn't want to go back to the hotel so he just wandered round for a while. He tried to think about the information Shane had given him. But he just wasn't feeling up to it. He cursed himself and wondered what he was strolling around for and what he was looking for. When he found the answer he cursed himself, went back to his room, emptied the bottle and went straight to bed.

He awoke with a headache. The sun was shining outside. It was already very warm. Kane looked at his grimy face in the cracked mirror. He had dark rings under his eyes. He made a grimace and reached for the water jug.

It took him three days to trail through every café, bar, hotel and saloon tracing somebody who could remember Peter Caine.

Without luck. It looked as if the three men had ridden into town, had gone straight to the bar, talked to Thompson and then followed him out.

Kane went over to the sheriff's office. Pickering had just been given a tray of coffee from the café across the street. He asked if Kane would like a cup. Kane said he would. They drank coffee while they discussed Thompson.

'Will you show me where Vincent was killed?' Kane asked after a third cup.

Pickering nodded. 'Now?'

'Sure, why not?'

The sheriff fetched his hat and gunbelt and took Kane to a small alley way between a large warehouse and a stable, now falling down and unused.

'I found him here. He was lying against the wall with both hands around this wooden bar here. Looked as if he was trying to pull himself up.'

Kane looked down at the place. Dust and odds and ends covered the floor. There was no sign of tracks.

'Was he killed exactly here?'

'Most likely. The blood had seeped three inches down into the ground beneath him.'

Kane looked at the planks in the fence. Pickering noticed it. 'If it's bullets you're looking for you can drop the idea. We went over every square inch. The murderer had definitely stood at the opening of this alley and shot inwards. There were quite a few who heard the shot. If the shot had been fired in here it would have been muffled a bit.'

Indisputable logic, Kane thought. He followed an imagined path the bullet would have taken from the entrance to the alley way towards where he was standing. The alley ended suddenly against a dilapidated fence full of cracks and holes. The bullet had most likely disappeared that way.

'I just can't understand what the hell he was doing in here,' Pickering said slowly, 'unless he was being followed and hid in here.'

Kane could have told him that it was impossible. Vincent was the kind of man who didn't run off without firing a shot. And his service revolver was found in his holster and hadn't been fired. There had to be another explanation. Another strange thing was the way Vincent had his hands around the wooden bar at the bottom of the fence. It would be more likely that he would die with his *revolver* in his hand. He could have been enticed in and shot at close quarters. He may have had an arranged meeting with someone he thought was a friend. Or it could have been an arranged ambush. Kane dropped the thought when he realised that there were too many solutions to the problem.

'These buildings around here,' Kane said, 'do they contain anything special?'

'No. We checked that.'

'Okay. Feel like a ride, Sheriff?'

'You mean to the place where Thompson was killed? That's okay by me, but cut out the "sheriff" bit. We know each other from way back, so don't be so formal. The name's Ed.'

Kane followed him out of the alley way. He'd have to change his opinion of Pickering and forget what he had once thought about him.

The sheriff left the office to be looked after by a deputy and they fetched their horses from the stable. The sun was high in the sky when they rode east out of town.

The place lay in a dried-out valley. Pickering stopped his

horse in a stony stream bed and looked around. 'We found him here.'

'Who found him?'

'A couple of boys.'

'Did they move him?'

'No, they were terrified and came straight to me.'

Kane studied the place. 'You find any tracks, Ed?'

Pickering pointed northwards. 'I found marks from horse shoes on the stones down the river bed here. He'd obviously ridden upwards. He lay right here, straight across these stones.'

'Where'd he bin hit?'

'Right side, just under the shoulder. The bullet went straight through him, even through his left upper arm.'

Kane nodded towards the ridge. 'The shot must have come from there.'

Pickering nodded. 'We checked the place. No empty shells.'

Damn him, Kane thought, he's got a no for all the answers. Loudly he said, 'The man who fired that shot wasn't far enough away for it to do that much damage.'

'I'd reckon on about fifty yards.'

Kane nodded. 'If the killer . . . ' He stopped as a thought suddenly struck him.

'Well?' the sheriff said impatiently.

'The murderer could have been close to him. Then the empty shell would be around here some place, in the river bed.'

They found it later. The empty cartridge case had slipped out from beneath a stone. Pickering whistled slowly. He looked at the shell in Kane's hand. '.44, eh?' he said.

Kane looked at the cap on the cartridge. The firing pin hadn't hit it dead centre. That meant that the firing pin was worn down or had been knocked out of line sometime. A very important detail. Kane knew just how much a ballistics expert could get out of an empty cartridge case. The ejector had also made clear marks in the shell.

'Anything against me looking after this, Ed?'

'No, by all means.'

'Okay, let's ride back.'

They separated outside the sheriff's office and Kane went back to his hotel. The light-haired boy waved eagerly at him.

'Telegram, Mr Kane! It says "urgent" on it!'

He read it in his room. It was from Shane himself. The telegram said,

JAMES WALDRON HAD A GIRL UP UNTIL TWO WEEKS AGO IN DODGE CITY STOP NAME PEGGY LAMAR STOP GIRL KNOWN TO BE AFTER ANYTHING SHE CAN GET STOP SUGGEST YOU CONTACT HER STOP SHARPEN YOUR SWORD AND GOOD LUCK STOP SHANE.

Kane crumpled the telegram angrily together and threw it at the wall. He sat down and stared at nothing. Then he lit a cigarette. He decided to head for Dodge City but was damned if he'd snoop around the slums and clip-joints after this girl Peggy Lamar. He intended to misunderstand Shane's ironical orders to 'sharpen his sword'.

Chapter 4

He rode north next day and took it easy all the way. He let the horse decide on the pace and he took in the landscape, dry, wind-swept. Clearly, a dry, early summer had forced the cattle farther south. Even the otherwise water-rich Carrizo Creek was just a muddy strip in the landscape. He reached North Canadian River the following day and found himself in one arm of the territory of Oklahoma. A few miles farther north and he rode into Kansas. Crossing the Cimarron River was easy too and the third day he caught sight of Dodge City – he saw the smoke hanging above the horizon. He hadn't been in Dodge City for some time. The town wasn't what it had been. Wyatt Earp had totally changed the character of the town before the famous fight in the O.K. corral in Tombstone, Arizona. Kane thought: it had been boom-time for the undertakers while Wyatt Earp wore his star in Dodge. Now – at the end of the eighteen-eighties the town wasn't better nor worse than any other society in the Middle West. The cattle boom wasn't seasonal now, as it was the years the cattle drovers followed the old Chisholm trail and the cowboys turned the town completely upside down. The cattle ranches lay adjacent now in south Kansas. They all bore a sign of industry now – the meat industry. The railroad increased enormously and mile after mile of cattle wagons rattled east all the year round, on the way to the canning factories and an insatiable European market. Dodge City was slowly shaking off the pioneer spirit and slowly starting the process that all prosperous towns go through – from the past to the present.

Kane felt sorry to see the old buildings derelict, the huge, ugly houses with their false façades and flashy signs. The streets were no longer muddy or dusty and full of ruts, there were poplars along the main streets and new signs with 'Stores' and 'Company' and 'Amalgamated'.

He passed the sheriff's office. It was a solid, low building made of logs, also with a couple of poplars outside now. The prison stood on the neighbouring site, a square, white-washed box of bricks. Even here were the inevitable poplars.

Kane made a face and turned his horse towards an old stable. He put his horse away and paid five dollars for brushing, hay and exercise. With his saddle bags across his shoulder he walked over to the hotel he always used in Dodge, an old, three-floored house with a weather-beaten exterior and a large, old-fashioned sign that said in carved lettering – 'Drifters Hotel'.

The streets were packed with people. Kane noticed that a great number of men were using high hats. It was a sight for sore eyes to see a real Stetson. Women's hats bore fantastic decorations of ostrich feathers and false flowers, and they wore large bustles that Kane thought ruined the natural form of a woman viewed either from the side or back. Light, elegant carriages with well-groomed horses slid quietly to and fro in the streets. Kane was surprised to see quite a number of single women driving their own carriages. That would have been unheard of just ten years before.

Kane walked across the street deep in thought. A sharp voice shouted something and a shadow in the street made him react. He had walked right out in front of one of the wagons. The black horse reared up and the woman in the driver's seat lost her hat as she struggled to calm the animal.

'Can't you watch where you're going, you clumsy idiot!' she shouted angrily.

Kane threw his saddle bags on to the pavement, grabbed the horse by its bit and dragged it down. He talked softly to it. Her hat lay just in front of the right wheel of the buggy. Kane made the horse take a couple of steps forward and to his joy saw the grotesque pile of cherries and roses squashed flat.

She leaned over the side. Kane looked at her as he stood holding the horses.

'Oh . . . my hat! You . . . you . . . clumsy oaf!'

Kane thought she was beautiful. He looked back at the

monstrosity under the wheel and backed the horse up. He picked up the remains and went over to the buggy's door. Close up she was maybe even more beautiful. She was blonde with a skin like a peach. She was so blonde that the down on her upper lip shone like silver in the sun. Her eyes were surprisingly nut-brown with flashes of gold. Her mouth – now narrowed in anger – was well-formed and the slight, angry dampness on her bottom lip made her even more attractive.

He removed his hat. 'I'm terribly sorry, ma'am,' he said, seriously. 'I was engaged in deep thought. It's been so many years since I was in Dodge that I hardly recognise the place. My name is Kane. I'm no fashion expert but if you'll allow me to buy you a new hat I guarantee you that it will suit you . . . ' He was about to say 'much better' but changed it, at the last moment, to 'well'.

She shook her head impatiently. 'Definitely not, Mr Kane. If you will be so kind as to let my horse go . . . ' She grabbed the whip and stared straight ahead. Kane smiled and leaned his elbows on the edge of the buggy. He said, 'I can afford it, ma'am. You don't have to feel beholden at all.'

Her mouth twitched but her voice was ice-cold. 'I cannot possibly accept a hat from a complete stranger. And now, if you'd be so kind as to release my horse . . . Mr . . . '

'Kane. Morgan Kane, ma'am. We aren't strangers. You know what I'm called. We've been conversing for some time.'

'*Too* long, Mr Kane. People will start to notice us.'

'Maybe a Paris model, Miss . . . Miss?'

'No, please go to one side . . . '

'I've just been out east. I can give you a good tip.'

She looked at him, at the dark, narrow face, the grey eyes, the high cheek bones and the finely formed mouth with the arrogant, almost brutal lines. But it was the eyes that made her capitulate, the clear, glittering grey eyes that danced with challenge and mockery deep inside like sparks.

'All right, Mr Kane.' She tapped the seat beside her. 'Jump in.'

He fetched his saddle bags and jumped up into the buggy. She managed the whip and reins like an ostler and Kane enjoyed the peaceful drive through the town and into a street where the shade from the trees brought a coolness to the buildings there. She tied the reins to the hitching post and turned towards him. Kane hadn't said a word during the minutes the trip had lasted and there was open interest and curiosity in her eyes.

'Here we are, Mr Kane.'

He looked at the exhibition in the windows. He nodded, opened the door and went in first. Then he took off his hat, offered her a narrow, brown fist to help her.

She laughed, quickly. 'You are most gallant, Kane.'

He just smiled.

An older woman and a youngish one – obviously her daughter – were unpacking some hats. Silky paper and ribbon covered the counter top.

'Hello, Edie . . . hello, Sally. This gentleman here has ruined my hat and has offered to buy me a new one.'

Edie was the older of the women. Kane noticed that she looked at him first before looking at the blonde girl. Her daughter, Sally, blushed and looked down.

'Couldn't have been a better time,' Edie smiled, her short, fat fingers unfolding the silk paper and putting three hats on to the counter – each one worse than the last, Kane thought. 'These came from "Sadie's" in Philadelphia. Got them today.'

The blonde girl sighed and began to try them on. Kane didn't know what to do with himself. He already bitterly regretted this hat nonsense.

Edie looked at them with a smile. 'What do you think, sir?'

He looked at the hat. It looked like an ant-hill overgrown with something that looked like violet threads. Three ostrich feathers formed a sort of fountain. A bunch of red and pink flowers were fastened at the foot of the feathers. A broad silk band – royal blue – was knotted beneath her neck.

Kane thought it was a monstrosity. He said so, too.

The women exchanged embarrassed smiles.

'I'll take this, Edie. Will you send it over to my place?'

'Of course, *Miss Lamar*.'

Edie turned to Kane and discreetly told him the price. He took out the money, watching the girl from one side. Something inside him wanted to laugh and laugh. His common sense told him that this *must* be the same girl . . . Peggy Lamar. Lamar was not a common name. And the first girl he met in

Dodge . . . Kane couldn't help smiling.

'Cheerio, Edie,' Miss Lamar said.

' 'Bye. In an hour?'

'Fine.'

Kane nodded to the women and followed her out.

'You have a most uncommon name, Miss Lamar,' he said, helping her up into her wagon.

'My father. He was French. The christian name is very common – Peggy.'

'Blonde hair and blue eyes are also unusual.'

'So I'm told, sometimes. Mother was from Scandinavia – that's where I got the hair.'

They drove a while in silence.

'Where are you staying, Mr Kane?'

'Drifters Hotel.'

'I'll drop you outside.'

'Thanks.'

Kane watched her from the corner of his eye. She concentrated on her driving for a while. He couldn't understand this. Peggy Lamar wasn't the kind of woman that one would associate with a bounty hunter. Maybe Shane was making a mistake? Could there be another Peggy Lamar in Dodge?

They reached the hotel. Kane noticed that her gloved hands were uneasy around the reins. He wondered if she was expecting him to make a pass at her. Most likely, he thought. But he wasn't going to move too fast in this. If she was the real Peggy Lamar he'd have to play carefully . . . as one does with waxed cards.

She stopped the wagon and turned. 'Honest, I've got a bad conscience, Mr Kane. I drove too fast, maybe. And you weren't to blame that my hat pin was too loose.'

'It's all been a pleasure for me,' Kane said. He climbed down and took his saddle bags out. He placed them on the sidewalk and took off his hat. Some of the black hair fell across his forehead. It gave him a piratical appearance. She thought he was strange, fascinating. And casual. She wasn't used to that. When she looked into his glittering eyes she decided to abase herself slightly to give him a chance – in case he was shy.

'You paid a high price for my hat. Would you rather not see it again?'

He answered calmly, 'I'd like to see *you* again – wearing the hat. But that cannot be today, I'm afraid. I've got twenty-five thousand head of cattle to sell before the banks close . . . '

She gasped. 'Twenty-five thousand . . . !'

He nodded.

'But . . . that's a fortune! The price is around twenty dollars now.'

'Twenty-one with horns and hoof,' he smiled, lifting the saddle bags. 'But maybe tomorrow, Miss Lamar?'

She was stunned. 'But that's over half a million! Are all those cattle yours?'

'Partly.' He smiled. 'Tomorrow?'

'Er . . . yes, thank you,' she said.

'Well, be seein' ya,' he said and turned to go. He hadn't got far when she shouted.

'You don't know where I live!'

'No, that's true,' he said, casually. 'Where *do* you live, Miss Lamar?'

She told him her address. He smiled and walked on. She said something unladylike and an elderly man was startled, passing by. She used the whip on her horses too hard and drove quickly up the street. Her cheeks were aflame with anger. She hated to feel that she had made a fool of herself. And that's how she felt now. Damn that handsome, arrogant devil! Peggy Lamar decided to cure him of any eventual silly ideas. She was an expert at curing men of getting the wrong, silly ideas. She told herself that Kane was just another handsome, self-assured fool with too many successful conquests behind him. But a slight tremor in her breast made her doubt it – doubt who would be the loser when the fight was over . . .

Kane placed his baggage in his room, ate a quick dinner in the dining-room and went down to the sheriff's office. A deputy told him that the sheriff wouldn't be at the office before six that evening, but he was most likely at home. Kane was given the address. The house lay just outside town and showed that the sheriff had earned well and used his money wisely. It was a large, white house with a small garden. Everything was surrounded by a low, white fence.

He knocked the door with the brass doorknob. A young girl

of about eighteen years opened the door. Kane asked for the sheriff.

'He's in his office, mister. This way. Let me take your hat.'

He thanked her and let her take his hat.

The girl knocked on a door, stuck her head in and shouted cheerfully, 'A man to talk with ya, daddy!'

'Send him right in, Kate.'

Kane smiled down into the green eyes as he walked past her. She paused before shutting the door behind him. It was a small room overflowing with books, papers, gun-racks and piles of stencilled sheets of paper. A heavily built man in his late forties got up from the pile of papers on his writing desk.

'My name's Kane.' He took out his silver star and let it shine in his hand.

The sheriff smiled. 'Leo Lanzing here.'

They shook hands.

'Sit down,' Lanzing said. 'Now what brings a state marshal to my dump?' He stuffed his pipe with tobacco and studied Kane through the smoke with sharp, green eyes. Kane thought of his daughter and realised that she had inherited her father's eyes.

He said, 'First I ought to tell you that I'm here on a real hush-hush job.'

'Got it.'

'I need a contract of sale written by a local cattle company that has been signed by yours truly. It's got to look real, genuine.'

'That can be arranged.'

'Twenty-five thousand head at twenty dollars and ninety cents per animal.'

'Quite a sale you've made there, Kane,' Lanzing chuckled. 'This something to do with cattle theft . . . rustlings, maybe? Oh . . . sorry, no questions!'

'I can tell you this much, that it concerns swindles with bills of sale,' Kane said smoothly. 'Hope to get them on the hook when I start waving this.'

Lanzing nodded. 'Is it urgent?'

'This evening if possible.'

'Old Silverton in the newspaper is a first class man with a printing press. I'll have everything ready at nine o'clock.'

'Thanks,' Kane said. He paused. 'Does the name James Waldron mean anything to you, Sheriff?'

Lanzing leaned back in his chair. 'Waldron,' he mumbled, 'Waldron . . . nope, can't say it does right now but if you give me a few details of how . . .'

'This doesn't have to have anything to do with this swindle,' Kane pointed out, 'it's something I'm just curious about. Peggy Lamar, a glamorous blonde here in town, was supposed to hang around with him I believe.'

Lanzing snapped his fingers. 'That's right! Peggy Lamar's a wild cat who runs a big house at the northern end of town, has a lotta parties, balls and such like. She seems to be swimming in cash and nobody knows where it all comes from. There's a rumour flying about that she got her claws in some old guy down in Missouri, who died real fast leaving everything to her. She's been in town for three years and is already very popular among the town's well-off bachelors . . . and among others in town who aren't so well off but hope to be soon.'

'And Waldron?'

'Belonged to the latter. A young, real handsome guy with gold on his Colt, the romantic type, his after-shave lotion smelled of horse. He was in her good books for a while, they were seen a lot together – especially in this new gambling den, "Queen's Heart". They kept it up for a month or so, maybe, then he just lit up and left.'

'Has he been here before?'

'Sure. Worked for a while for a mining company down by the border, called himself the security officer. In my time that was just a hired guard, handy with an iron.'

Kane got up. 'Thanks for the help, Sheriff. I'll be back around nine then?'

'Come down to my office, Kane.'

'I'll do that.'

'Kate!' Lanzing bellowed.

The door opened. 'Yes, daddy?'

'Show Mr Kane the way out.'

Kane fetched his hat. It smelled of roast meat in the corridor. Kane felt hungry. He couldn't resist sniffing the air.

'Roast neck,' the girl said. 'Like it, Mr Kane?'

'I only eat beans,' he answered seriously. 'Goodbye, Miss Lanzing.'

She watched him go, one finger in her mouth, standing there until he had gone through the gate. Then she went back in. She thought he was handsome and exciting but perhaps a little too old. She was glad she hadn't invited him to dinner. Daddy wouldn't have liked it, maybe.

Kane slept for three hours, washed and shaved, changed his shirt and went down to the sheriff's office at five to nine.

Lanzing gave him the papers. The mysterious engraving expert in the newspaper office had done a superb job. The document stated that the 'Dodge Cattle Company' had bought twenty-five thousand head of cattle from Morgan Kane, St Louis, Illinois, at a price of twenty dollars and ninety cents per animal. The sum was to be transferred over to 'Kane Cattle Ranch's' bank in St Louis as soon as possible. The other paper was a receipt for transport of the same amount of animals from the 'Western Union' railroad company.

It was magnificently done, with signatures, and had been stamped. Even the place where the stamp had slipped slightly and made a smudge looked very convincing. Kane mentioned this.

'Had to fill in a little here and there,' Lanzing chuckled. 'I think it sounds okay saying you're from St Louis. I hope you don't dislike the town. This town sends between two and three million head of cattle to St Louis each year and your supposed number will just drown among all those.

' "Dodge Cattle Company" doesn't say much. The company exists but it's just an amalgamation of cattle ranchers who operate freely inside the union they've formed. I suppose it's a sort of a club. A sort of OK stamp for quality and honest dealing. I think these papers should see you through as long as they're not checked *too* closely. I'll guarantee the stamps and signatures on 'em, if nothin' else.'

'I hope this guy Silverton doesn't get any ideas of changing our dollar bills,' Kane chuckled.

'I'll just have to let him,' Lanzing said. 'He's too good for me . . .'

'Well,' Kane said, 'thanks for all the help. I'll keep you informed.' *If* Peggy had anything to do with that gang these papers would show that he was just a rich cattle man interested in a lovely girl. Kane liked to be sure.

It had started to get dark outside and the street lights were on. The town glittered with light. Kane pushed the papers into his inside pocket and started off down the street. Soon he was in a street with poplars on each side. It was a quiet street. He stared in through the open gate. A gravelled drive led up to a large, white house in southern-states style, with balustrades, pillars, garden paths and a summer house. Two lamps on each side of the main door lit up the façade and after a while Kane realised that the house wasn't as big as it seemed. He could see it by the doors. They were, in comparison, enormous compared with the rest of the walls and width of the house. A miniature palace, he thought, studying the dark garden at the back of the house. Through the big french windows he could see the light of many chandeliers. He was sure he could make out couples dancing in there. He listened. Yes, he could hear the music now.

Peggy Lamar was having a party. Curiosity got the better of him and he crept down the dark garden. He walked around the house and counted six buggies, equally as elegant as the one she used. Three dark figures sat on a bench talking to each other. Most likely drivers.

Kane walked back. He found the road leading to the town centre again and realised that the town must have grown at least fifty per cent during the last ten years.

He stopped uncertainly outside the hotel but didn't feel like sleeping. He knew he'd be lying awake thinking of her. He wondered if he should kill time with something. 'Something' right now meant a woman. No – not that – it would be best to be in tip-top condition the following day. Cynically, Kane thought about Shane's advice of 'sharpening his sword'. That was just what he was doing – by steering clear of it.

He thought of the 'Queen's Heart' – the gambling saloon where Waldron and Peggy had hung about. He asked a passer-by and was told where it was. Just on the edge of town. All the new buildings were farther out.

Kane started to walk. The thoughts of gambling put him in a good mood.

Chapter 5

The place wasn't very big. There were two saloons, each about a hundred and twenty square feet and divided by an arched door covered by heavy velvet curtains. The floor carpets, curtains, upholstery, table tops – everything was covered by red velvet. Even the expensive, silk wall coverings had blood-red hearts instead of the usual golden French lilies. All this red gave the room a sickly, almost nauseous tone. All the other colours were drowned. There was something unhealthy about the room. The guests seemed unhealthy; their eyes reflected red. Their hands were pink, almost like the jellyfish Kane had seen in the Gulf of Mexico.

Two waiters in dark red livery took his hat. Kane noticed that they both gave him curious, searching looks. When he saw the two narrow gunbelts hanging on pegs in the wardrobe he understood. He slapped his hips.

'No weapons, gentlemen.'

'Right, sir. Welcome, sir. Perhaps you'd like to change some cash now?'

Chips, Kane thought, and definitely red. No green here which would ruin the atmosphere.

'Yes, thanks.'

One of the men waved to a young, effeminate looking man wearing the same dark red costume.

'This gentleman wants chips, Joe.'

A glittering smile. 'This way, sir.'

An elderly man stood behind the counter. Kane changed two thousand to ten and hundred dollar chips. As he expected – they were red. These had various sizes to differentiate between their worth, whereas usual gambling chips had various colours. Apart from that they bore a 10 and 100 figure in discreet gold numerals.

The effeminate Joe breathed down Kane's neck.

'Which game do you prefer, sir?'

Kane moved away from the perfumed character behind him.

'Poker,' he said, briefly.

'There's an empty place in here, sir.'

Kane followed him into the other room. He felt sick watching the man's twitching hips and the way he slid through the curtains covering the doorway. The other room was a perfect copy but in here there were only five-men poker tables.

Only three of the tables were in use and only one was full. Joe pulled out a chair where three people were sitting . . . two men and a woman . . . the minimum in poker playing.

'Sir?' Joe asked, questioningly.

'Morgan Kane.'

Joe bowed to the woman. 'Miss Tennison.' Then he turned to the men, two elderly men with hard faces, dollar signs for eyes and a glance for Miss Tennison's deeply-cut dress. 'Mr Hawk and Mr Russell.' Effeminate Joe stopped the introductions with a greasy smile and with a 'good luck, lady and gents,' wriggled away again.

Kane breathed a sigh of relief and sat down. The men gave him the once over, glad that a fourth man was joining in. Better choice of cards. The chance of a good hand was better and a bigger kitty.

Kane nodded – a nod that was meant for everyone, and placed the chips in front of him. He ordered a glass of whisky and a jug of water and cut with the others. It was Kane's turn to deal. He shuffled calmly, making sure that his fingers didn't work *too* easily but not too lightly. In poker Kane chose the middle road – then he had sway on both sides.

He met Miss Tennison's glance when he gave her the first card. It was only for a second but Kane couldn't remember the last time he had received such an open invitation. She had clearly been bored to tears with the other elderly men. The other women at the neighbouring tables had captured all the young men so Kane realised with a cynical smile that he must have come like manna from Heaven and nectar for her soft, female pride.

He returned her glance with added interest and was given a tiny, red tongue-tip in reply. Everything was fixed there so Kane picked up his five cards. When he saw the three aces, two red and a black one, he knew it was going to be okay and that the fours flanking the aces couldn't be better. Nothing could go wrong now, with the red-haired Miss Tennison's slim leg against his, the whisky golden in his glass with a hint of red, and the slippery cards between his fingers that were now trembling with sensitivity.

Kane knew now that he was sitting with a fantastic lucky streak – a lucky streak that a professional gambler experiences about once every ten years. It was up to him now if he was going to leave this red nightmare with a fortune in his pockets. Lady Luck had touched his knee. He had only one thing to do – keep his cool while she held him there.

Four hours and seventy-two hands later Kane looked down at the pile of chips and discovered that he had won twenty thousand dollars. He had a bitter taste in his mouth after smoking the thirty cigarettes he had, and a slight, warning pressure behind the eyes from the five glasses of whisky and water. Still, he was not tired in the least, his brain was crystal clear and his eyes seemed clear and wide open, without the stinging pressure of tears that usually followed after hours of concentration, smoking and drinking.

Two other gamblers had joined them. The table had started to attract onlookers. Now there was a woman in her fifties, a Mrs Arden, and a young nervous man with a pimpled neck and red, bony hands. His hands resembled sick crabs in the red light.

Kane looked at his cards. He had a line of queen, jack, ten, nine and a smaller diamond. Usually Kane didn't draw for a straight but right now the 'straight' was 'open', at both ends, so he threw in the diamond. It cost him a hundred dollars to buy the single card but Lady Luck was still holding his knee and dished him a king. As there were five playing there was a great chance that someone or other had a hand that would top his 'straight' . . . a flush or house was enough. But Kane – sure that

Lady Luck was with him – pushed the odds up to eleven thousand dollars, forcing two of the players to throw in their hands, and paid three thousand more to 'see' Mrs Arden. Kane beat her three queens and cashed in for about fifteen thousand dollars.

Three of the others pulled out. It was almost three in the morning and only the young man with the pimples and Miss Tennison still carried on. Kane cleaned out 'pimples' for another three thousand by betting on everything he had and the young man tried to bow casually as he got up – flat broke.

He smiled into Miss Tennison's flashing, reddish-brown eyes.

'Looks as if there's only us two left,' he said.

'I can't follow up, Mr Kane. Your luck and method of playing is . . . overwhelming.'

'One more hand?' he said lightly, shuffling the cards. A couple of waiters went round blowing out the lights, and screwing them down.

'I haven't got enough money.' She pushed a long, red finger nail among the small pile of hundred-dollar chips she had in front of her.

'Haven't you anything to bet with, Miss Tennison?' Kane felt a purely physical contact with her eyes. He saw that she understood his meaning and he saw the way she paused – trying to think what to answer – and how.

'Do you see anything of value that corresponds to that fortune there?' Her eyes seemed to sink into his. Kane felt a pressure in his stomach. This was the last cut of the evening and then, snap, down from Lady Luck's lap. If only she wouldn't let him down in this last gamble! He shoved the pile of chips across the table, staring into her eyes the whole time. His own glittered like rubies in the red light. Her breasts rode and fell quickly in the low-cut dress.

'I'll bet all this . . . on one thing, Miss Tennison,' he said.

She gasped. 'But . . . what can I bet against that?'

'Yourself!'

The tongue-tip was there again. Her eyes had a greedy expression. Excitement made her even more desirable. Kane could hear his own heartbeats.

'One cut,' Kane said softly. He put the cards on the table.

'One card each, highest wins.'

She looked directly into his eyes. 'What if you lose . . . ?'

'I'll take the chance.'

The tip of her tongue was there again. 'Just to have me?'

'Yes,' he answered.

Her hand began to shake. It neared the cards in jerks. Then – suddenly – the trembling left her. It was an adult, self-assured, proud woman that divided the pack and lay her card down.

Jack of spades.

Kane just snatched his cut carelessly and showed her the lowest card in the pile. He read it in her eyes, the mental surrender, the female unconditional surrender to the male.

The queen of hearts. Lady Luck had given him a final kiss of farewell.

Kane looked at her through half-closed eyes. She stood naked in silhouette against the dawn that lit up the thin curtains. He knew she was standing there purposely. She wanted him to see her.

Kane lit a cigarette. He lay on the bed smoking a while. His body felt pleasantly empty and relaxed. He wondered how he was going to begin.

'It's years since I was last here in town,' he said quietly. 'I should have come sooner.'

'I've only been living here for two years,' she answered coquettishly.

Kane made a grimace in the semi-darkness.

'Must say the town's changed. I was almost run over by a young woman. A very attractive young woman,' he added.

As expected she was suddenly curious – perhaps slightly jealous.

'Oh, how'd she look?'

'Fair. Blonde – with brown eyes . . . I think.'

'You certainly got an eyeful of her!'

'She seemed . . . different,' he said, casually.

'She *is*.'

'Know her?'

'Yes, she's called Peggy Lamar.'

'She lives here in Dodge?'

'Yeah, keeps a big house in southern style. We were friends until . . . up to a while ago,' she answered and then walked over to him. She sat on the bedside and stroked his hard, muscular body. Her sensitive finger tips noticed the uneven skin.

'My God, you're full of scars.'

He said, 'What were you quarrelling about?'

'Who said we were?'

'Two beautiful women in one town . . .'

She laughed. 'You're an expert at flattering, Morgan. Where did you learn it?'

'I've got long ears. Tell me what happened, Moira.'

'Does it interest you that much?'

He shrugged. 'Like I said – she almost ran me down.'

'All right.' She lay against him, her head on his shoulder. Kane stroked her back, almost absent-mindedly.

'We were good friends for a while,' Moira Tennison said. 'We were at parties, picnics – we were very popular. I had a friend then, a very handsome man. We had even discussed marriage. Well, Peggy Lamar went after him. And Jim, well . . . he was no better, no worse than other men.'

Kane smiled in the semi-darkness. Lady Luck still hadn't let him go yet.

'What happened then?' he mumbled sleepily.

'I told Jim to get to hell out of here. Peggy took him after me, played with him a while until she was tired of him and then kicked him out.'

'That's life, Moira.'

She stretched in pleasure. Her skin shone like satin in the weak light. 'I'm glad now though. There were rumours that Jim was mixed up in some dirty business. He came less and less to Dodge.'

'What do you mean by "dirty business"?'

'I'm not sure, Jim never mentioned his work.'

'Jim,' Kane said lazily, 'that's another way of saying James, isn't it?'

'Yes. He's called James Waldron.'

'I think I've heard of that name,' Kane said. 'In connection with a swindle.'

'I'll bet. Let's not talk more about Jim. How long will you be staying in town, Morgan?'

'Depends. Difficult to say. Depends on a woman.'

She clawed him slowly with her nails. 'What woman, Morgan?'

'She's called Lady Luck.'

She bit his ear and cheek. 'What does she look like?'

'I've never set eyes on her.'

'You a gambler, Morgan?'

'In a way.' He turned towards her. 'This Waldron – does he ever come into town?'

She stiffened. 'Why do you ask?'

'Wouldn't like to run across him in your place.'

She laughed and pressed herself against him. 'You won't. Sometimes he comes and mews around Peggy but she just throws him out.'

Kane's thoughts went back to Shane. How in hell could he know that . . . He dropped it. Moira was breathing heavily in his ear. He grabbed her by the hair and twisted her head into the angle he wanted it. He kissed her brutally.

Chapter 6

My God, Kane thought, as he shaved himself in front of the mirror that same evening. He stared at his face with disgust. He cursed Shane and the lucky contact he had got for him. He had slept for five hours then he had had some water and a bath brought up and he had taken a bath. After a couple of drinks he dared to use his razor. He washed away the soap suds, threw water in his face and reached for the towel. He hit the soap and it slipped down under the bed. Kane began to swear, angrily. Then he just had to get soap in his eyes – and swore even more.

After a while he got dressed and sat quietly in the armchair by the window. He was thirsty so he took a couple of swigs from the bottle and gasped for breath. Then he had to laugh at himself. What in hell are you complaining about, he thought, you have been sleeping with a beautiful woman and have just won a fortune. You've found out where James Waldron is and you've got an appointment with another beauty in an hour's time. Once you would have dreamed of this situation!

He glanced at the holster that lay on the bed. Should he wear it? Old habit made him grab it. He routinely flipped open the cylinder and checked the chambers. Then he checked the hammer, the working parts, slipped it into his holster in the top of his trousers. He took another drink and wondered if he should use the same methods on Peggy Lamar. He doubted if the two friends would meet during the day and doubted even less that they would exchange intimate details about each other's private lives.

Kane chuckled. He felt better now. It was half past seven

when he donned his lightweight dark jacket, tied up his lace tie and put on his flat-crowned Stetson. He locked the door behind him and went down the stairs.

He walked slowly through the busy streets and reached her house around eight o'clock. He lit a cigarette and stood in the shadow of the gate post and smoked a while. There was light showing in two of the ground floor windows. The first floor was dark.

He trod on the cigarette butt and walked up the gravelled drive. Instead of a door knocker there was a bell rope. Kane pulled it. He heard a melodic clang far in the house. Kane pulled a face . . .

A grey-haired Negro opened the door. He was dressed in a costume that had been used twenty years previously on the plantations.

'Mistah Kane, suh?'

'That's right.' Kane gave him his hat and walked into the hall. It was not too large but had carefully chosen furniture. Woven carpets covered the tiles and brass candelabra threw a warm light across the oak panelling.

'Miss Lamar is waitin' for yuh in the salon, suh.'

Kane couldn't help chuckling. He followed the bent, old jewel down the hall and into an impressive salon.

'Mistah Kane, Missus,' the old jewel said and closed the door silently behind Kane.

Peggy Lamar got up from a low sofa, a French one, Kane guessed – covered in silk cushions. It suited the style with which she offered her hand for him to kiss and Kane thought it quite natural to kiss it gently.

'Mr Kane, how pleasant!'

He stood there looking at her. She was quite a sight in the dark, low-cut, old-fashioned lace dress. Her blonde hair had been swept up and covered by a pearl-covered hair net. She wore a simple gold chain around her neck on which hung a nut-sized emerald that dangled between her high breasts. The narrow waist on the dress accentuated her hour-glass figure.

'Sit down,' Peggy Lamar smiled. 'Or would you like to look around first?'

'I've seen just about all I want to see already, Miss Lamar.'

'Peggy.'

'All right . . . Peggy.'

'A drink, Morgan? You'll find whatever you'd like on the tray over there. Pour me a glass of wine, would you please?'

Kane chose a dark red wine for her. He chose a whisky for himself – Harper's Old Kentucky Tavern. He filled the glasses and went back to the sofa. A fire blazed in the fireplace. A couple of crystal chandeliers glittered in the light. He looked into her eyes above his glass.

They drank deeply. Kane put his glass on the carved, nut-wood table beside the sofa. His eyes glanced around the dimly, softly lit room.

'You've got a lovely home, Peggy.'

'It doesn't seem as if your own home in St Louis matches it, Morgan.'

'A camp full of men,' he smiled.

'Oh . . . no woman?'

'No woman.'

'How did the sale go?' She put down the empty glass and Kane went over to fill it.

'Great,' he answered with his back towards her. 'Twenty dollars ninety per head.'

'Plus thirty thousand in the "Queen's Heart"!'

Kane turned slowly. 'Rumours fly fast around here,' he said, calmly.

She smiled. 'Are you surprised?'

'Yes.'

'You mustn't be, not when Moira Tennison is sitting at the same table.'

'Oh? Do you know her?'

'I *did*.'

Kane sipped his whisky. He was getting tired of these cats mewing at each other. He drank a little more. 'Well,' he said, 'now it's over and I can go back with a good conscience.'

'What's over?'

'The sale.' He looked at her through narrowed eyes. What was she trying to say now?

'How was she, Morgan?'

Kane put down his glass and moved towards the door.

'Wait!'

He stopped and turned. His eyes were ice cold.

'I'd like to apologise. It's just that . . . well, Moira is a bitch. She's always trying to . . . to . . .'

'Yes?' Kane said mildly.

'All right, get everything from me! She wants to get revenge for a stupid incident that happened some way back.'

'An incident called James Waldron,' Kane said.

'Did she tell you that?'

'She only mentioned it.'

Peggy leaned forward. The emerald sparkled. As she opened her mouth to speak Kane heard voices coming through the door behind him. He moved quickly to one side when he heard quick footsteps and the door flew open with a crash and a man rushed into the room, stopped a few paces inside the room with Kane behind him.

'Jim!' Peggy Lamar exclaimed. 'What do you want here? Get out of here!'

Kane saw a shudder pass through the man when he realised that Peggy's guest must be standing behind him. His right arm began to shake slightly.

Kane said, 'That's right, Waldron, I'm standing behind you.'

The man turned slowly. Kane saw that he was around his own age, a well-built, handsome man with clear-cut features and dark hair. A silver buckle shone inside the half-open jacket.

The Negro whined in the open doorway. 'Couldn't help it, Missus, Mistah James is too strong for me.'

'Get out of here, Julius,' Waldron sneered. 'Who's your guest, Peggy?'

'Jim, you must be drunk to come rushing in like this,' Peggy cried, angry and afraid. 'I've told you that you're not welcome here any longer!'

'I asked who this man was?'

Kane said, 'The name's Kane.'

'Where'd ya pick him up, Peggy?' Waldron said, thickly. 'Couldn't ya stand sleeping alone any longer?'

'How dare you . . . you . . . you crook!' Peggy shouted, leaping to her feet. Waldron backed away until he could see both of them. Kane met his eyes. His scalp tingled when he realised that Waldron was about to draw any second.

'Take it easy,' he said coldly. 'No reason to make a lotta trouble.'

'Get outa here,' Waldron said, thickly. 'Ya hear, Kane . . . get the hell outa here!'

'*You* get out of here,' Peggy shouted. 'Morgan is my guest!'

That was enough. Waldron spat, his lips taut and white, 'Then he'll have to be carried out!'

His hand flew inside his jacket.

Kane's shot stopped the movement. Waldron screamed and whirled around. A nickel-plated revolver shone in the light before falling to the floor. Waldron grabbed his right arm with his left. Blood trickled out between his fingers.

Kane's ears were still ringing. He flipped the barrel of the revolver upwards. 'Kick the gun under the sofa, Peggy. Open the door. I'm taking him to the sheriff.'

She was pale and trembling. 'Are you coming back?'

'Open the door!' Kane snapped. He saw that Waldron was about to throw up.

She quickly opened the door. 'Tell Julius to drive your carriage up to the door, fast,' Kane went on. 'And I mean *fast*!'

Peggy rushed out into the hall. She shouted to Julius.

Kane looked at Waldron. He was green around the gills with shock and pain. The carpet was absorbing the blood that dripped from the lame fingers.

'I need a doctor,' Waldron said hoarsely. Pearls of sweat ran down his face.

Kane didn't answer.

Peggy opened the door. 'The carriage is ready.'

'Out,' Kane said. Waldron took a couple of unsteady steps. Peggy grabbed Kane by the arm. 'You're coming back?'

'Yeah,' he said impatiently.

Waldron staggered down the garden. Kane stayed four paces behind him. He knew what cold night air could do to a shock-dulled mind.

Without warning Waldron whirled around. His boot flashed towards Kane's crotch. But he'd misjudged the distance between him and Kane and missed completely. Kane smashed him across the head with the butt of his Colt. Waldron grunted and sank to his knees. He tried to creep forward. Oaths and curses poured from his distorted mouth. Kane let him come close. Then he really whipped the butt of his gun across Waldron's head, hard and fast. The man sank like a sack, unconscious. Kane dropped the revolver into his holster and bending down, grabbed the man by the belt, pulled him up into a standing position and then flipped him across the shoulder. He carried him down to the carriage, threw him in, climbed up on the driver's seat and grabbed the reins. Not long after that the carriage slipped quietly out of Dodge City on the way to the uninhabited desert stretches towards the east, where the 'Western and Union' railroad chugged along beneath the dark sky.

Waldron sat leaning against the wheel of the carriage. He was tied up to the spokes of the wheel with lengths of rein.

Kane sat on a rock in front of him and smoked, waiting for him to regain consciousness. He was tense, excited. By a miraculous stroke of luck he had got hold of one of the most important members straight away. It was up to him to get the truth out of Waldron now. Kane's thoughts went back to another dark night – on Cuba – when he had also sat in front of a man and would do to him what he was later to relive in dreams. Kane dropped the thoughts. To hell with false sentimentality!

He hit Waldron across the face with his own hat. The man moaned and blinked. The clouds parted. A ray of moonlight entered the gully. Up above them on the embankment stood telegraph posts, like gallows along the railroad lines.

Waldron's face was clearly lit. He said hoarsely, 'What in hell's goin' on?'

Kane picked up a stick lying beside him and hit the man with it.

A roar of rage and curses.

Kane hit him again – and again.

Waldron began to whine, quietly.

'Just to show that I ain't kiddin',' Kane said, swallowing the disgust he felt. 'You're gonna talk, Waldron, talk fast too. About Peter Caine, Tom Conway and the bounty hunting you're all working on – everything. Get it?'

Tears and spittle ran down Waldron's distorted face. 'You can go to he . . . !'

Kane went to work with the stick again. Five minutes later

Waldron began to talk. Ten minutes later Kane was on his way back to town. He stopped outside the sheriff's office. A deputy talked with him, went to get the sheriff and look after Waldron.

Kane had a quiet talk with Sheriff Lanzing. Waldron was placed in a cell and someone went to fetch a doctor.

Some minutes later Kane left the sheriff's office. He rode down to the telegraph office, woke the man on duty and sent a telegram. It said:

PETER CAINE THE LEADER. JAMES WALDRON BEHIND BARS. GANG HAVE HEADQUARTERS IN PAMPA – EAST OF AMARILLO. HEADING THERE.

Kane paused when he came so far. Then he added: SWORD WAS SHARP ENOUGH. He signed it and asked the telegraphist to send it as soon as possible.

Kane packed his things, fetched his horse from the stable and was out of Dodge City as the sun rose.

Chapter 7

Kane knew where Pampa was. It was a small, dying cattle town, killed by its livelier neighbour – Amarillo. The town was situated in a landscape that was best suited to cattle – on a smaller scale. There was very little of that now, the hundred or so inhabitants lived off the people travelling from Amarillo in the west and Oklahoma and Tulsa in the east.

Kane considered what James Waldron had told him. Was that everything? It seemed *too* simple – that the gang contacted bounty hunters and offered to trace the hunted man, organise the hunt, help them in every possible way – for a payment of twenty per cent of the takings. But should there be any more than this, really? No. Done in this way, with good contacts over the whole of Texas, there *had* to be more rewards. And it was a fact that most of the wanted men got out – to Mexico maybe, or left the country completely. The way the hunt was now being organised a wanted man didn't stand a chance. Of course the payments on these men would increase. And Peter Caine was the brain behind it – the man who organised the spy-net, made contacts where county sheriffs and judges lived, places where they were always sure of new, genuine information. Waldron and Conway were trail dogs – the ones who sniffed out freelancers and enticed or threatened them into or out of the organisation. They also took care of the killings. Sometimes someone or other would get greedy and want all the reward money himself. It didn't take the organisation long to find him and liquidate him.

Kane thought about the job Waldron had been given, to contact a man called Marlow in Dodge City – a man he *hadn't* met. This Marlow was a man – according to Waldron – who had been a lone wolf farther north in the country – a man who was known throughout four states for his merciless traffic, a man whom Peter Caine had hoped to recruit. And, Kane thought, what is more natural than I take his place? He hoped that Marlow lay dead somewhere or other. And if he rode into Dodge, right now, a day or two late, he would never know that his contact, Waldron, lay in the town's prison. The real Marlow would wait a little, decide that he'd been fooled and leave the town – without even knowing what the offer was. Kane considered the plan from end to end. It was as perfect as it could be. And if anything went wrong . . . He shrugged. He had managed to get out of impossible situations before. There was only one thing he was worried about and that was Waldron's job *after* he had contacted Marlow. Should he *personally* follow the new recruit to Pampa? Or had he other assignments to cover – assignments that wouldn't be covered now and finally would go against Kane in the long run.

Kane sat bowed in the saddle and stared down at the thin column of smoke that thinned out eastwards in the hot, dry wind. He had reached Pampa. Things would clear up now. He spurred his horse down the slope, where a few skinny bulls leaped aside.

Washing blew cheerfully from a washing line on the edge of town. A group of hens pecked and scratched in some dry horse manure in the street. A couple of tumble weeds rolled along in the wind. A door slammed somewhere. There was something dilapidated, dead, nasty about Pampa. Kane felt it in every nerve, as he rode down the town's only real street and saw the faces weighing him up from the filthy windows he passed.

He tied up his horse in front of a bar, knocked the dust off his clothes and glanced quickly up and down the street. He concentrated on his rôle as Lew Marlow, professional bounty hunter.

The bar was dusty and dirty and stank of old tobacco fumes and liquor – cheap liquor. A couple of poker games hardly bothered to raise their eyes. They ducked behind their greasy cards.

A fat, filthy man in an even filthier apron moved slowly towards Kane.

'Yeah?' The voice was coarse, bad-humoured.

'Beer.'

The thick brew spilled as the glass was placed in front of him. Kane stared into the bartender's blood-shot, unhealthy eyes.

'I asked for a beer, mister.'

'You got it.'

Kane took the glass and tipped it. He emptied the contents behind the bar counter. The bartender's eyes turned round with anger.

'A glass of beer,' Kane said mildly. He felt that the poker players had turned to watch the excitement. It was deathly quiet in the bar.

'You can go to hell,' the bartender said between his teeth. He opened a flap in the counter and came out. His trousers were wet with beer. Kane saw that he was a big man but fat had won the race over muscle. But he was big enough and strong enough to beat him to a pulp if he let him.

'Lick the beer off these trousers or get the hell outa here!'

Kane rolled the butt of his cigarette between his finger and thumb. He flicked it into the bartender's face just as he was about to hit him. The hot end caught him beneath the eye. With a roar he raised his hands to his face. Kane watched him with interest. The man dropped his guard and rushed at Kane like a bull. The heavy fists swung wildly and would have crushed Kane's head if it had been there. But he dodged lightly backwards. The tip of his boot lashed out and caught the bartender just beneath the knee cap. The man roared with pain. He was out of his mind with anger when he limped towards Kane again. Kane was sick of the whole business. He feinted twice then shot out a fist to the man's gut. Then he dodged to one side, passed the crouched body, and stretched his hand stiffly like an axe blade. The blow struck the man across the neck like a club on a bull's carcass. The man's eyes closed instantly, paralysed he began to collapse and Kane helped him inside the opening in the counter with a vicious kick. The bartender hit the wall with a crash that shook the whole room.

Kane looked at the poker players. Not one of them raised an eyebrow. Kane walked calmly behind the bar and found a barrel of beer. He filled a mug, placed fifty cents on the counter and went over to a corner. He pulled out a chair, put his feet up on it, pulled the hat down over his forehead. He sipped his beer, watching the poker players. They looked away. After a while one of them got up, put on his hat and made for the door.

On the way to Caine, Kane thought, drinking more beer. His hand ached and he regretted using his right hand without thinking of the consequences. He stroked the revolver butt. He had put his Wayne Martin holster on a normal cartridge belt. The holster was tied to his thigh with a black elastic cord. Kane knew that with the holster placed like this he could draw and fire in roughly two-fifths of a second. He had a feeling that maybe he'd need it soon. He massaged his right hand beneath the table. Minutes passed. Then he heard voices outside.

Just then the bartender suddenly got up. Kane found himself staring into the black, twin barrels of a shotgun. He literally leapt up from his chair and fired faster than perhaps he'd ever done before in his life. His Colt roared while the hammers on the shotgun were falling. Both barrels thundered and the shot grazed Kane's left shoulder and hit the wall with a crash. The bartender's head was thrown backwards. The bottles on the shelf behind his head were splintered and with a gush the contents sprayed out. Kane's eyes were empty with shock. Gunsmoke from his revolver rose around his body. The bartender's heavy body slipped down on to the pile of broken glass. The swing doors opened. A small, slim man dressed in a dark suit and hat stood there, staring from Kane to the space in the row of bottles and the shotgun that lay across the bar. The barrels were still smoking.

'Well, amigo,' the man said. 'Quite a mess. What happened?'

'Jake turned the shotgun on him,' said the poker crowd.

The small, grey man looked admiringly at Kane. He started to walk slowly across the room. Kane saw the bulge under his jacket on the right side. He said, 'I'd keep your hands away from your sides if I were you.'

The man stopped dead. His eyes looked yellow. His breathing was heavier. It was a clear warning and the challenge was in Kane's tone of voice and the man's reaction told Kane what he wanted to know . . . he was a gunman.

'Who are you, stranger?'

'Name's Marlow.'

The yellow light disappeared. The man smiled, a narrow, weak sort of smile.

'Nice to meet you. I'm Tom Conway. We've been waiting for you.'

'Oh yeah,' Kane said.

'Let's go.'

'I ain't finished with my beer yet.'

The smile disappeared. 'Then drink it!'

Kane sat down and drank the beer in four slow gulps. Conway stood and stared at him the whole time. After a while Kane put down the glass and grabbed his hat.

'You first, mister,' he said, threateningly.

Conway laughed. He turned on his heel and walked out into the street. He pointed. 'The hotel, okay?'

Kane just nodded. He was still shaken. Like everyone he was terrified of a shotgun at close range. It had just been a question of an inch or two and his left arm would have been lying on the floor. A horrible thought! He looked at the jacket sleeve. It had been torn, the lining and padding showing through. A stinging told him that a few pellets had grazed him. He felt something warm down by his wrist. A thin trickle of blood oozed through the dark hair on the back of his wrist.

Conway turned. 'Where's Waldron?'

'You the boss?' Kane snapped.

'Why the hell you askin'?' The voice was angry.

'Since you're doin' all the askin'.'

Conway barked his short laugh again. That short bark of laughter Kane was going to hate before long. It told him of Conway's temperament. Quick reaction, short fuse, restless energy – all the traits that made him dangerous with a gun in his hand. Kane stored it for a future date.

The hotel foyer was dusty, empty and falling apart. Conway went up the stairs first. He turned to the right and knocked on the first door. He opened it and looked at Kane.

'Go in then, man,' he said impatiently.

Kane showed his teeth. 'You first, mister.'

'Stop these childish games,' said a deep voice inside the room. 'Come in, Tom – and you too, Marlow. This hotel isn't as empty as it seems.'

Conway barked again. Kane followed him into a small, grubby room. A man sat on the edge of a bed, his face turned towards them. A revolver with an octagonal barrel was carelessly pointed at them. Kane opened his mouth to say something but the man on the bed beat him to it. With a sharp click the hammer fell – on an empty chamber. Kane felt the sweat break out over the whole of his body. He met the ice cold eyes over the strange revolver. The thumb drew back the hammer again. Kane knew instinctively that a .38 bullet lay under that hammer – and he had Conway behind him. How in hell could he have believed that he could bluff these boys?

Then a surge of hot anger filled him. His eyes narrowed to glittering flecks and his teeth appeared through a vicious mouth. He hissed: 'Just you pull the trigger, mister – but bet your last dollar you're gonna join me on the hell train!'

The finger jerked as the hammer fell. Kane drew – but not quite conscious of what he was doing. Conway's revolver had already knocked him on the head. His Colt 'Police' Special slipped out of his fingers and Conway grabbed him before he hit the floor.

The man on the bed pointed the revolver at Kane and pulled the trigger eight times after each other.

Eight sharp clicks.

With a burst of laughter he put his hand inside his jacket and took out a handful of bullets. He started to fill the chambers with nine bullets.

Conway was pale and sweating. 'Come on, Peter . . . one day and it ain't gonna be as you planned it! You're playing this game too far! What if he'd managed to draw and fire?'

Peter Caine stared at Kane, unconscious on the floor.

He said, 'I trust you, Tom. You know that.' He started to laugh. 'Tie him up and put him in that chair.'

When Kane came to he was tied up in the heavy chair. Tom Conway and Peter Caine had pulled the bed out on to the floor. They could reach him if they leaned forward slightly.

Kane was dizzy with pain. He felt sick in his throat but forced it down. His eyes cleared.

'First,' Peter Caine said mildly, 'before we do anything else, I want you to answer a few questions for me. Every time you lie I'll knock out one of your teeth with this here.' He stroked the long-barrelled, strange revolver. 'You get that?'

Kane met his eyes.

'Yes,' he answered.

Chapter 8

Peter Caine had kept his christian name. His real name was Peter Shabarov. He was Russian by birth and had escaped with his parents, during one of the Tsar persecution acts, to the north, through Russia to a port where some American seal hunters had been offered a fortune in jewels to take them to America. Peter had been eight years old then and his memories were vague about what had happened. He remembered the cold. He had never felt worse pain than the icy, paralysing, killing cold of north Russia. Even now – in his forty-eighth year – he still had the cold in his body. He never opened a window. He never removed his jacket. He used long, warm underwear even in heat waves. It seemed as if his body absorbed the heat, used heat to stay alive. He bathed in water that would have scalded other people. He slept under blankets and eiderdowns that would have suffocated others in sweat.

Like many other Russian refugees, his family settled in Boston. The town had contacts with the fishing town in north Russia famous for seal hunting until the hunting grounds were finished and Nova Scotia and Newfoundland became the new centres.

The family had had few difficulties in settling due to the valuable items their father had taken with him. After a while the Shabarov family became respected – mainly because of their wealth. Alexander Shabarov had the biggest estate agency in Boston before the Civil War and the stately house he built in the town's best snob area told everyone that the Shabarov family were there to stay in their new fatherland.

Peter had hated his father as far back as he could remember,

To him his father was just a dark, thin man, a stranger that was both God and Devil, judge and executioner in one and the same person. The hardness, disregard and brutality that had brought him the huge sums on the stock market in the eastern states, all this Peter had felt personally. His father tried everything to create a *better* copy of himself, a piece of hardened steel that would carry on the Shabarov name forever. Peter was too young to understand that the memory of the shameful flight tortured the proud Russian aristocrat every minute of the day. Marina Shabarov – his mother – was raped eleven times on board the ship as they were sailing in a heavy storm and his father lay unconscious after being hit on the head by a spar from the rigging while trying to help the crew to furl sails. He didn't know that his father with his own hands had strangled and buried in the garden the result of that horrible stormy night. Marina Shabarov never appeared officially again after that and rumour had it that she was mad. Someone had heard her howl at the moon on stormy nights. Others had seen her wander restlessly round in the garden shouting, shouting – as if she was looking for a child....

Peter grew up in a house full of emptiness and nastiness. He took his father's punishments with the same patience that made him put up with the hour-long lectures on the future of the family, the way toughness and willpower won through whereas to be weak and the underdog was to be forgotten, dead – things that made no impression on his boyish mind.

When he was old enough his father placed him in West Point. Young Peter should – as his father had done – complete a military education and become an officer, as his father had been in the Tsar's bodyguard. But the hard discipline made Peter sick. Route marches and physical exercises he could put up with to a degree – but not the cold. He froze every minute of the day. The single blanket the cadets were issued with could never hope to satisfy the abnormal need for warmth he felt.

It ended with him stealing a couple more blankets.

He was kicked out of the school in dishonour.

It was that evening when he came home – a bitterly cold winter evening – that his father broke his nose with one blow, then lashed him with a riding crop until his lean body looked as if it was dipped in red paint. Alexander Shabarov renounced his son that night, renounced his existence and threw him out of the house – out into the cold.

For ten years Peter lived in the Boston slums. He begged, robbed, stole. He developed the invaluable qualities that criminals often develop, intelligence, quick-thinking, courage – in a way, bravery. But these remarkable qualities were directed *against* the society, against those that *had* something and were different.

One day the time came when he was caught and put in prison. He was given two years for theft and those two years removed the last of the warmth in Peter Shabarov. When he was released from prison he headed south – towards warmer climes. He practised until his accent was almost unnoticeable, and he changed his name. It didn't take him long to contact other criminals in Texas. He became known as a cold-blooded, often reckless desperado who, after a while, other gangs had use for. And Peter looked after his money. His cold, clear mind sucked up every impression, every experience. It wasn't long before he tried working with his own gang. They started carefully, petty theft – a couple of calves. A couple of years later he stole four thousand head of cattle in West Texas and sold them in Mexico. It was the biggest cattle theft up to that date east of the Rio Grande. Later followed swindles with gold in California, robbery of post wagons and money transports, robbery of wage carriers to the railroad camps, also the theft of jewels from the railroad too. Quite a few of the train robberies that Jesse James had been blamed for were done by Peter Caine. Then came gun running to the Indians after the Civil War, when tribe after tribe broke out of the reservation and stormed the badly manned forts in the western territories.

Unlike other big criminals, Peter Caine knew that one day he was going to stop it. He placed the whole of his fortune – about one million dollars – in safe investments in eight states. He bought a ranch and hired the best people he could get and became immediately an unknown, rich and slightly eccentric rancher in the north of Texas. Later – when boredom and the lust for adventure were unbearable he began to work on a new idea, a hobby, legal, exciting where there could be a lot of money.

One day he came across a hobo, by chance, on his ranch. The man fired at Caine without warning. He missed but Caine didn't. When he took the body into town he was, to his surprise, paid five hundred dollars. The man was wanted for murder and armed robbery.

Caine considered it. Five hundred dollars for a three cent bullet meant. . . .

A plan began to form in his mind.

And now – three years after, as he sat staring at the man tied up in the chair – the plan had brought him almost a hundred thousand dollars. And this man – Marlow – could help him to raise that sum quite a lot. Caine knew that sooner or later he would be found out. He had set his aim on a million and a half before travelling to Europe . . . for ever. All he needed now was the extra hundred thousand. He needed Marlow. The thirty-five thousand he had found in Marlow's money belt proved it.

Caine was used to judging people, in his cold, calculating way. He knew right away that Marlow was a man who could not be described as being normal. He knew it from three things. First, Marlow's reaction when he thought he was going to die. Secondly, the hard, bone hard will-power that showed in the grey eyes. The third was the lean, scarred body. There was satisfaction in his eyes when he looked into Kane's eyes.

'Mr Marlow,' Caine said pleasantly, 'I didn't arrange this meeting because I like playing. It was no game when I pointed that revolver at you.'

'It might have been a dangerous game,' Kane sneered. 'Why am I tied up? What the hell's goin' on here?'

Caine raised his hand, impatiently. 'One moment, Marlow. I want some questions answered. Where is James Waldron?'

'No idea,' Kane snapped.

'But you spoke with him?'

'Sure! At the hotel.'

'And then?'

Kane sighed with impatience. 'He said what he was sent to say. He was drunk. He babbled something about a woman he wanted to get his hands on. Don't remember the name. Peggy something-or-other. He said he'd be back at the hotel the day after and ride here with me.'

'Well?' Caine leaned forward.

'He didn't come. He was still sleeping with this woman when I saddled up and rode. To hell with him – I don't waste time on no womaniser!'

Caine pulled the sleeves of his dark, thick jacket down over his wrists, as if his hands were cold.

'You seem to lack understanding, Mr Marlow? Hasn't anything similar ever happened to you?'

Kane sneered, 'Like hell!'

'What . . . don't you like women?'

'They're useful,' Kane said brutally. 'But they've got a tendency to hang on a man's shooting arm if it goes too far.'

Caine and Conway exchanged glances. A smile appeared in the corner of Caine's mouth.

'You're most likely right. Well, Waldron will be along – meanwhile you're wondering why we asked you to come here.'

'You can say that again,' Kane snarled.

'It is a business offer, Mr Marlow. An offer that – if you accept it – will bring you fifty thousand within six months. And – I will emphasise the fact – is all legal.

'We found exactly thirty-five thousand in your belt,' Caine went on. 'I hope you will forgive us. How long have you worked for that money?'

Kane's face was a study in anger because of the ransacking of his belt and the greed that showed. 'Round five years.'

'Aha!'

Kane shut up and looked down. Had he managed it? Did they believe him? The exchange of glances when he had mentioned Peggy's name had done the trick maybe. There was no doubt that Waldron had mentioned the blonde beauty in Dodge. He was that type. Kane had taken the chance that Caine had also discovered that.

'Fifty thousand, Marlow?' Caine said quickly. 'Are you with us?'

'I never play reckless – unless I've got the ace high!'

Caine laughed. 'No, I'm sure of that, Marlow. But to come to the point . . . your line is bounty hunting. We can more or less deliver the biggest sums on a plate. The only thing you have to do is to fetch the reward. With, of course, a percentage to us.'

'How much?' Kane tried to lean forward in eagerness.

'Twenty per cent. With the men lined up for you this should bring you about . . . let's say fifteen thousand in six weeks.'

'Get these ropes off,' Kane said.

'Not so fast! Are you with us?'

'Bet yer bottom dollar I'm damned well with ya! But on one condition – or ya can drop the whole affair 'sfar as I'm concerned . . . I hunt alone.'

'That's okay, Mr Marlow. And now, when we let you go, would you mind forgiving us for the hard treatment we have given you? The whole thing was arranged to give us a clearer picture of you. We are very careful when we choose people to work with.'

'That's all right,' Kane said.

The ropes were cut and Kane started to massage his hands and wrists. Caine placed the revolver on the bed. Kane looked at it.

'I ain't seen anything like that before.'

Caine laughed quietly and with satisfaction. 'That's understandable, Mr Marlow. There is only one example – *this* one.'

Kane didn't need to play curious. 'Can I look at it?'

When Caine nodded and delivered the pistol butt first, Kane relaxed. This was the final sign that he had been accepted.

While Kane studied the revolver he had Caine's slow, boring voice in his ear the whole time. There was something foreign about the way he talked.

'In 1877 Smith and Wesson factory were asked by the Russian Tsar if they could produce a revolver for the Tsar's bodyguard. You have perhaps heard about it? The factory took eight months to construct a model and it was passed as suitable. Up until then this revolver – Smith and Wesson "Russian" – was the best handgun that had ever been made. A few examples were sent out of the factory and are worth a thousand dollars each. Well, *this* revolver, Mr Marlow, is an improvement on the Smith and Wesson "Russian". A famous gunsmith in Illinois – his name is of no importance – got hold of an original "Russian" and using that as a prototype he built a new one, using my own ideas.'

Kane weighed the weapon in his hand. His eyes were full of admiration.

'As you may know, the original was a .44 calibre. I chose a

.38 and by strengthening the cylinder there was a space for three extra bullets. This is likely to be the only revolver in America today of this calibre that has nine chambers in the cylinder. Notice the construction, Mr Marlow, which has also been strengthened to balance the extra chambers. I chose an eight-sided barrel – to be honest a crib from the European Nagant revolver – because it gives more surface and therefore better cooling properties. The bullets have a charge which is fifteen per cent stronger than the normal .38 calibre gives. Therefore the extra strengthening and for ballistic reasons the barrel had to have exactly one and a quarter inches added. The butt is a mixture of Colt and Smith and Wesson – the best qualities from each model. The butt plates are made from African India rubber to give maximum friction for even a sweaty hand. Well, Mr Marlow, do you like the gun? I may as well tell you that the gun cost me between three and four thousand dollars, the "Russian" model included.'

'It's a beauty,' Kane said, and he meant it. The gun was heavy and long-barrelled but the balance was perfect.

'The balance was made to suit my hand especially, and my wrist, taking into consideration the strength in my forearm,' Caine said. 'I doubt if you could draw this gun faster than your own. Personally I have drawn at a speed at a little under two-fifths of a second.'

Kane stared at him. Could it be possible? Something in the eyes before him told him that it was true. It *was* possible.

He said slowly, 'That's real fast.'

Caine got up and went over to the window. 'I have always made sure of staying anonymous, Mr Marlow. The fact that Peter Caine's name has never been mentioned in the same breath as John Wesley Hardin, Doc Holiday, Bat Masterson and Buck Duane doesn't change the fact that I am most likely the fastest gun in the country at the moment.'

Chapter 9

Later that day Kane lay on his bed in the hotel and blew thoughtful smoke rings at the dusty ceiling. He couldn't deny that he was excited. Up until now it had been *too* smooth. He was right in the middle of the gang and had the gang leader just two rooms away from him. The thought of drawing on Caine and Conway had passed through his mind. He doubted whether he could take them both. But he wanted to draw in the net, get a glimpse at the spy net that covered the three western states where the gang operated.

He had eaten dinner with Caine in the hotel's surprisingly elegant dining-room. During the dinner Kane was given his first assignment – he was to ride to a small, nameless town just south of the border and 'fetch a reward' of eight thousand dollars. The man was called Smiley Whittaker and lived in a small shack on the edge of town. He had been there for three weeks. The town had no idea of his identity. The population, Caine explained, was twenty per cent Mexicans and half-breeds.

When Kane asked why *he* should do the job Caine answered that this Whittaker was reckoned on as being a very fast gun, a psychopathic killer who already had seventeen notches on his gun, not counting Mexicans. Caine said that he couldn't just ride up to the hut and gun him down. Whittaker was always on his guard. It wouldn't be easy to take him.

Kane had agreed. Eight thousand was a sum that *Marlow* would risk his life for. Kane had no choice.

He grabbed the bottle on the table and took a swig. He thought of Caine – and his two-fifths of a second draw. It was a fraction of a second faster than he was. Kane didn't bother to worry about it. There was little chance that he and Caine would meet in a face-to-face gunfight. And he knew that if ever they did start fighting he would kill Caine like a mad dog – in any possible way. He was a U.S. Marshal, not a gunman polishing up his reputation.

Caine had also said that Whittaker's body was to be taken to Dalhart. The gang had made sure that Whittaker was wanted in that town, and that the marshal there could check the details with the county sheriff in Amarillo by telegraph.

Kane decided to ride through Amarillo and send a telegram personally. Something told him that eight thousand was a high price to pay – even for a killer of Whittaker's reputation.

Kane saddled up the following morning. Caine came out on to the stairs and offered him a rifle.

'A present, Mr Marlow.'

It was a brand new Winchester 73. Kane pushed it into the saddle holster along with his own rifle.

'The trip will take you about three days. I'll be expecting to hear from you in about two weeks. When you've received the money you ride here to Pampa. Got it?'

Kane bent over the saddle horn. 'Okay.'

Caine smiled. 'And you wouldn't be so dumb as to think you can ride around Pampa? Do it, and *your* price will be ten thousand, Mr Marlow.'

Kane straightened up. 'I don't need threats!'

'Just a warning,' Caine smiled. 'Good hunting.'

Kane swung into the saddle and spurred the horse. He saw Tom Conway in an open window. The little gunman watched him with a strange look on his face.

Kane shrugged. He let the horse have free rein towards the north-west. It was great to be in the saddle again.

The following day he reached Amarillo, after a day's hard riding. He put his horse away in a stable and went into the first and best cellar café and ate a solid meal. He tried to make out that he wasn't being watched. Maybe he was just nervous? Kane was sure that nobody had followed him. But the gang could have given his description to contacts in Amarillo, in case he did something he wasn't supposed to. He was smart enough to reckon on being watched. And whatever he did now had to look natural.

Kane smiled as he paid the bill and walked out into the busy street. He made his way to a cheap hotel, hired a room for one day and paid six dollars. Then he stripped and slept until the evening.

It was getting dark when Kane entered the first bar and emptied four glasses of whisky, one after the other. Then he leaned across the bar and waved a ten-dollar bill under the barman's nose.

'Listen, friend,' Kane said slightly slurred, 'I'm heading off again soon, long trip and thought maybe I'd pay a visit to a . . . house . . . here in town? Where is it?'

'Hobart Street. Number eight. Say Pete sent you.'

'Thanks.'

Kane walked stiffly, with a couple of small stumbling steps occasionally until he came to Hobart Street. It was a dark street where the houses lay back from the street.

He opened the gate to number eight and noticed that the windows were dark. The house was empty – and the bartender could expect a hiding – or the windows were covered with curtains that didn't let out the light.

Kane knocked hard with his knuckles. He waited a little and knocked again. The door was opened and a huge mulatto in a dark shirt and tight leather trousers stood there. Kane stared into the unhealthy, yellow eyes.

'Watcha want, mistah?' the giant grunted. Kane guessed that he must be the bouncer, a muscle-man that fixed any drunks who got too drunk or eager.

'Pete sent me,' Kane said, rustling a bill in his fingers.

The mulatto backed away. 'Come on in, mistah.'

Kane went into a semi-dark passage. A staircase led up to the next floor. The few pieces of furniture there had worn felt coverings.

'Yer gun, mistah? You'll get it back when yuh leave.'

'I ain't here to do some shootin',' Kane said.

'That's the house rules, mistah.'

'Er . . . all right,' Kane mumbled, and took off his gunbelt. The mulatto put the belt in a cupboard and locked the door. He said, 'Twenty-five dollars . . . in advance.'

'What if I don't like the girl!'

'You just *betta* do that, mistah . . .'

Kane mumbled to himself and took out the dollar bills. The mulatto counted the money and nodded.

'This way, sir.'

Hm, Kane thought, suddenly I'm called 'sir' now!

They came into a room, filled with the same worn furniture and in semi-darkness. Five women sat there. Four white and one dark-skinned – most likely Mexican.

The mulatto gave him a key. 'Number four on the first floor, suh.'

Kane took the key, feeling slightly ridiculous. He'd been in a brothel before, where the system was more elegant than this – in New Orleans, for example.

He pointed to a small, plump, dark-haired woman.

'You,' he said, and turned and walked out.

The girl jumped up. 'Don't you want a drink first, mister?'

'No,' Kane said. He opened the door and went out into the corridor. He could not see the mulatto anywhere. The stairs creaked beneath him. The girl's dress rustled behind him. He came to a door with a card showing the number 4. He opened and let her go in first, then he locked the door and looked around.

It was a small, grubby room with a chest of drawers, a stand with a jug of water and a bowl, a broad iron bed with brass balls on the posts, thick, ragged curtains and red shades on the lamps.

Kane pushed his hat to the back of his head and took a good look at her. She wasn't too bad, face a little too broad but a funny, turned-up nose, blue eyes and a pretty, red mouth.

Resignedly, she began to take off her dress. Kane sat and rolled a cigarette while she did so. He wondered how to go about it. She was almost naked when he decided how to do it and couldn't help feeling bad about it when he saw the way her breasts hung and swayed as she walked over to the bed.

Kane sat on the edge of the bed. She lay back and looked at him. After looking at him for a few seconds a smile appeared on her lips.

'Christ, mister, what the hell are *you* doing here?' she said. 'I know a lot who'd pay to get into bed with *you*!'

Kane said roughly, 'What're you called?'

She raised her arms to him. The colour of the hair in her armpits told him that she was a natural blonde.

'Milly. Hey, why don't you strip?'

He pushed her arms away. 'Listen,' he said sharply, 'you want to earn twenty dollars?'

'Wow, you bet!' A speculative look appeared in her eyes. 'Why . . . you want special treatment?'

'Exactly,' Kane said. 'For twenty greenbacks you just lie real quiet here while I climb through that window over there and stay away an hour or two.'

'Christ, man, you must be outa your head! You mean *I* get twenty dollars while *you* disappear through the window?'

Kane tried to be patient. 'Listen, Milly, just forget about my state of mental health. I've offered you twenty dollars to lie here until I come back. Yes or no?'

'Yes, you bet! But what's the hurry?' She smiled invitingly to him and let the blanket slide down. If she says 'Wow' or 'Christ' once more I'll throttle her, Kane thought. 'Can't it wait just a little?' she said.

Kane went over to the window and pushed the heavy curtains aside. He looked out over a dark backyard. Without turning he said, 'Just stay right here until I come back, okay?'

'Okay.' She pulled the blanket up to her neck and looked disappointedly at him as he struggled with the window. After a while he got it open and crept behind the curtains. He sat there, waiting for his night vision to come. It was not more than maybe twelve feet down, but he took a good look before he jumped. After walking a hundred yards he swung out into a parallel street. There were few people in the dark streets. He kept to the shadows and was sure that nobody had seen him when he eventually stood outside the telegraph office.

A young man in a black alpaca jacket sat dozing behind the counter. A green eye shade gave his face a sickly colour. He looked up when the door shut behind Kane.

'A telegram form,' Kane said.

'Right away.'

Kane moved further along the counter. He thought for a moment, licked his pencil and wrote:

WHITTAKER. PRICE EIGHT THOUSAND. IS THAT CORRECT. LEW MARLOW, BOUNTY HUNTER DODGE CITY MUST DISAPPEAR A WHILE. WAIT FOR ANSWER. KANE.

He pushed the form through the hatch. 'Get that off as soon as possible. Address it to Mr Shane, Fort Leavenworth, Kansas City. I'll wait for a reply.'

'Right.' The young man read quickly through the telegram and sat down at the table. His right hand tapped out the message at lightning speed. Kane rolled a cigarette. He smoked that and three others before the answer came.

PRICE ON WHITTAKER IS CORRECT STOP LEW MARLOW WILL BE REMOVED STOP SHANE

'Three dollars seventy, Mister Kane.'

He paid and left. Well, that was that. He would have betted his last dollar that the reward was false. Damn it, was there no proof that the gang was doing this thing illegally? Kane trudged back to the brothel. There was nothing else to do except pay Whittaker a visit. If he wouldn't be taken alive then he would have to be killed. Kane didn't like the taste of this sort of dirty job. Whittaker had never done him wrong and he had never killed in cold blood. Whittaker was wanted by the law, that was for sure, and Kane would *for* the law – but that wasn't enough.

He came to the back yard and piled a couple of boxes on top of each other up against the wall. He climbed up, got hold of the window ledge and pulled himself up. The window was still open. Kane put his feet down carefully behind the curtains and peeped out. The girl was asleep with her mouth half open.

Kane took off his jacket and hung it over a chair. He rolled a cigarette and wondered if he should go back to the hotel. Don't be so bloody prudish, he thought. That bed's okay and broad enough for two.

He undressed and lay down beside her. He put the ashtray on his chest and smoked a while. Already the sheriff would be told, in Dodge City, to arrest Lew Marlow. If he wasn't already in town the sheriff and his men would search for him. Kane felt relieved now he didn't have to worry about Marlow suddenly making an appearance.

Kane yawned. He put out the cigarette, put the ash tray on the floor and turned over on his side.

When he awoke the girl was lying snugly up against him. During the night she had put her arm across his chest. Grey light revealed tears in the carpet by the window. Kane wondered how he could get up without waking her. He tried. The girl mumbled something and put both her arms around him. With a satisfied sigh she slept again. Kane swore silently. He noticed that he was beginning to react to the nearness of her body. She woke up half an hour later. A pale sunbeam struck the washing bowl. The curtains moved in the breeze from the open window. She looked at him, her eyes heavy with sleep. 'You came back,' she whispered. 'You really came back. I didn't think you would. I didn't think I'd ever see you any more.'

'I've gotta go now,' he said, quietly.

She pulled him against her. Her soft fingers began to fumble with him.

'Not yet. Please, not yet!'

'I must!'

'Is it because . . . you paid?'

'N-o-o.'

'If I give the money back to you . . . then you'll stay? Then it's okay? Say it's okay.'

'All right.'

Kane followed the railroad northwards to Denver, before heading more towards the west. He knew more or less where the town was, west of Stratford, by one of the many tributaries of the North Canadian River. He rode all day and camped when it grew dark. He sat by the dying fire until the stars twinkled coldly down at him. Kane wrapped the blanket around his shoulders. He wondered how he could avoid killing Whittaker. He decided later that it was pointless making plans. He made a bed of dried grass and used his saddle as a pillow. The horse stood some way away. Sleep just wouldn't come. He tried to keep thoughts from creeping into his head, he tried to just lie and wait for sleep but it was no use. Most people experience the same feeling now and again – during the day –

or night – when doubts and fears begin to worm their way in, when experiences, situations and people suddenly appear in a different perspective and a connection between them all appears. Kane had it that night. He suddenly felt that his nerves were cracking up. He thought of Peter Caine, Tom Conway, the unknown Whittaker . . . any one of them could be the person who was a fraction faster than he was. Any one of them could have that added amount of mental strength that would cause the balance to tip one way. He thought of the long line of men he had killed, the countless fights he had survived, he thought of all the people he had coldly and cynically exploited, betrayed. Glimpses of women. The way she brushed the hair from her eyes. The smell of hair. The taste of a kiss. The special, melting, drowning feeling of a woman's embrace. The sound of sobbing. The echo of his own cynical laughter.

Kane sat up, soaked in sweat. He tried to tell himself that there was no such thing as fate, that a person sooner or later has to pay for his misdeeds. It was a lie that Nemesis would settle the balance. It wasn't true that a person who *caused* pain would himself *feel* pain. It was ridiculous believing that a greater power balanced the accounts and suddenly caused the books to balance out evenly.

He lit a cigarette with trembling hands. It slowly left him . . . as it always had earlier. He knew that death had touched him and passed on.

Kane was up in the early dawn. His eyes stung and he felt heavy and tired. An empty feeling in his stomach told him he was hungry but he couldn't eat anything. With a curse he pushed his hand into his saddle bags and took out a metal flask of whisky. He was disgusted with himself for drinking and felt even emptier in his stomach when he felt the effect of the whisky.

He neared the small town in a dangerous mood. He wanted to challenge the thoughts that had plagued him during the night hours, prove that they were lies and he was just overwrought. He was cool, concentrated when he caught sight of the small, poor village down by the river bank.

A man called Whittaker was down there.

Kane suddenly knew that he was going to kill this man, just as the liquor had killed his own horrible thoughts.

Chapter 10

Kane didn't ride straight into the village. He rode in a circle around it until he had the place weighed up and knew how the shacks there were positioned. He saw a group of young girls – four of them – washing clothes down by the river. They beat the wet clothing against round stones. They were dark, with straight, jet-black hair.

Half-breeds.

Kane rode slowly and carefully along the river bank so as not to frighten them. They saw him from a distance. Dark eyes stared at him in fear and wonder from beneath the black hair.

He stopped the horse about ten yards from them. He raised two fingers to his hat in greeting. It wasn't answered. They continued to beat the clothing and stared and stared. Kane dismounted and led his horse the last few yards down to the water. He rolled a cigarette while the horse drank. He pulled up the horse's head before it drank too much. Then he knelt down and poured water over his head.

The girls stared. The beating action grew less and less. Finally they leaned back and sat on their heels, just staring, ready at a moment's notice to rush off. They were like deer with the smell of danger in their nostrils.

'Ah,' Kane said. 'That was great!' He wiped water out of his eyes and chuckled at them. 'Well, ladies – have you never seen a white man before?'

They didn't answer.

Kane led the horse over to them. He stopped just before they turned in desperate flight.

'You all look so frightened,' he smiled. 'Is something wrong?'

He laughed. 'You don't need to be afraid of me. I only want water. I'll soon be on my way.'

The oldest of the girls – she was about fifteen – began to relax. The flat nose and high cheek bones made her look years older. The black eyes glittered.

'We are always afraid, *señor*,' she answered in broken English. 'If you are hungry I can get you some food.'

Kane smiled and shook his head. 'No thanks, I have just had food.' He squinted at the girl through the cigarette smoke. 'You said that you're always afraid. Why?'

The girl's black eyes looked down. There was something in her face that made Kane shudder. Hatred? No, not that. Something else . . . something indefinite. He stared at her.

'It's not *you*, *señor* . . . it is your skin,' she answered.

The other girls began to moan and rock to and fro. It was a horrible sound. The oldest glanced quickly towards the village.

'There is a man in the village,' the girl said quickly. 'A white *diablo*-devil.'

Kane's eyes narrowed. 'Get up,' he said.

The girl looked at him. She slowly stood up. Kane saw her big stomach. She must be about eight months on the way already.

Then the others got up. The youngest couldn't be more than twelve or thirteen years old.

They were all pregnant.

Kane felt the sudden urge to kill flow through his veins. He had difficulties in speaking now.

'Why haven't the men here killed him?'

'They were killed, *señor*. They tried last year.'

Kane was startled. Last year? Whittaker had only been in the village a few weeks. There must be two different men.

'How long has he been here?' he asked.

'Since last winter.'

'What's he called?'

'*Señor* Whittaker.'

Kane made a grimace. It gave him a dangerous look. One of the girls began to cry. The others stood there, apathetically. Kane could understand, in a way, how a strong and sadistic nature like Whittaker could terrorise a small village. It had happened before.

'I'll help you,' he said. 'In what way can I be of assistance?'

'*Kill him!*' It came as a scream from them.

Kane looked towards the town. He could make out the nearest house where the river turned. There was smoke coming from the crooked chimney.

'Where does he live?'

The girls began to gabble as one. Kane grabbed the oldest one by the arm and shook her. 'Where does he live?' he snapped.

The girl backed away from his touch. Kane dropped his hand. He repeated the question.

'In the middle of town. In a stone house. Everyone had to help build it.'

'Does he ever go out?' Kane asked.

'Seldom. He just lies around drinking.'

'Is it possible to get up to the house without being seen?'

'Yes.' The girl's eyes brightened. 'Do you mean this, *señor*? Will you really kill him?'

Kane felt a jolt of pain in his chest. 'Yes,' he answered, emptily.

The girls began to chatter again. Kane asked a couple more questions before leading the horse down along the river bank and around the bend.

The clothing was beaten against the stones in an excited, almost wild rhythm.

It was dusk in town. The tumbledown shacks were dark. Light appeared only from the low, stone house in the middle of town. A yellow splash out on the dusty street.

Kane stood behind a corner and listened intently. He hoped the plan worked. He knew he would never get into the house. The door was solidly built, the girls had said. Whittaker had built it the previous year after one of the young men had tried to get in and kill him. Only women and old men were left in town.

Kane looked at the wall of the house. There was a sort of porch built of stone slabs outside. A person standing there would make a clear silhouette. The distance was fifty yards. Kane gripped the Winchester and tried to breathe normally.

Then he heard it!

'Señor! Señor Whittaker!'

It was a young girl who shouted. The voice echoed to and fro between the shacks. Kane had no idea where the shout came from.

'*Señor* Whittaker! A woman . . . a girl . . . *a white girl*! She is sick, *señor*! Sick!' Then not so loud, as if the girl spoke to herself, 'Madre Dios, she is so beautiful!'

The door was suddenly opened and Kane raised this rifle to his cheek.

Damn it! The door opened *towards* him! He couldn't see the man at all.

A rough voice bellowed, 'What the hell's goin' on? That you, Lia?'

'Yes, *señor*! Quickly, she is here . . . at Juan's hut. She must have hurt herself – she is almost naked! Her feet are bleeding, she must have walked far!'

It was getting darker. Kane swore when he realised that if Whittaker ran across the open square it would be too dark to shoot.

Then he saw a movement!

Kane took aim. It was too dark! He daren't shoot at the dark object moving quickly across the square. Kane dropped the rifle and drew his revolver. He ran silently after the dark figure. He heard Whittaker shout between the huts.

'Christ, Lia – where in hell are ya? It's as dark as hell here!'

Then, quieter, 'Here, *señor*! Hurry, she is trying to get loose!'

Kane ran towards the sound. It was only a question of yards now. Was Whittaker armed?

The voice was so near that Kane was startled.

'Lia! Strike a light!'

Kane stopped dead and peered into the dark alley way. He could make out a silhouette. How far away was it? Ten yards? Thirty?

He started to walk.

'Here, *señor*!' It was the girl again. Kane heard Whittaker grunt somewhere ahead of him. Suddenly the silhouette disappeared. Suddenly a light flared, so near that Kane shut his eyes against the glare. Someone had lit a torch in the narrow street.

Three things happened at once. Lia screamed, 'Kill him, *señor*!'

In the same second Whittaker swung around and Kane was startled to see how near the killer was. Thirdly, a revolver spat fire from Whittaker's right hand at the same moment Kane fired from the hip.

'Damn you!' Whittaker howled, his mouth distorted in a grotesque grimace.

Kane stood, feet apart, and fired round after round into the huge body until the hammer clicked on an empty chamber.

As Whittaker fell the torch went out. Kane stood in the darkness, his breath coming in gasps. He had heard the bullet whine past his head and knew that death had touched him again.

Then lights appeared everywhere – torches, lamps – the street was packed with people who sang and danced and hugged each other. The crowd moved into the alley way and the shouts of joy suddenly turned into animal-like screams as Whittaker's bloody body was suddenly lit up in the torchlight.

They threw themselves over the body like a pack of wolves.

Kane ground his teeth. He loaded and fired three times into the air.

The echo bounced angrily off the walls. It was suddenly very quiet. They turned and looked at him. Then they formed a ring. Whittaker and Kane were the centre of the ring.

An old man said: 'What is it, *señor*?'

Kane cleared his throat. 'I've got to take him back with me. He's a criminal. There is a reward for him – a price on his head.'

'We have belonged to him for two years, *señor*,' the old man said. 'What is more natural than he belongs to us for *one* night.'

'I need the body as proof,' Kane said hoarsely.

The ring edged nearer. Kane felt the stench of animal fury coming from them.

'Take it, *señor*,' the old man said. 'You have weapons. Take it!'

Some of the young girls edged forward. Their enlarged stomachs made strange shadows in the torchlight.

Kane looked at them. He looked at the old women. Then the old men. Then he dropped his Colt into his holster and said quietly: 'He's all yours . . .'

A terrible cry rose into the night air. Kane could smell the hate that was in the air. Their animal instincts had taken over now. Two years of hatred, fear, pain was now finding relief.

Kane backed away from the crawling, bloody pile. He turned his back and tried to roll a cigarette. The old man came up alongside him. Kane cursed and threw away the ruined cigarette paper. His hands were shaking too much.

'Don't despise us, *señor*,' the old man said desperately. 'We are perhaps animals in your eyes but if you knew what this village has suffered then you wouldn't condemn us so easily.'

'I'm not condemning you,' Kane said.

'They are like children now,' the old man said. 'Let them get their revenge. Let them become humans again, then a thing like this will never repeat itself. Another time they will *kill* themselves. They *need* this rotten human blood to wash away their own shame and powerlessness.'

Kane looked into the old, wise eyes.

He said, 'Has Whittaker ever left the village?'

'Never farther than the river.'

'Are you sure, *señor*?'

'Completely sure.'

Kane nodded.

After a while the crowd began to disperse. The alley way was empty. Triumphant voices still echoed through the streets a while, then all was quiet.

Kane stood there alone. A couple of torches still lay in the dust burning. He walked over to the spot where Whittaker had fallen.

There was only a few bloody strips left, half buried in the bloody earth. A terrible smell arose from the street.

Kane staggered over to the nearest wall, put out his arms to support himself and spewed like he had never done before.

Two days later he rode into Amarillo in the middle of the night. Without looking either to the left or right he rode straight down to the telegraph office.

The same young man was on duty. He nodded pleasantly to Kane. He recognised him again, obviously.

It took half an hour before the answer came.

Kane read it:

FIRST REWARD MARCH EIGHTY-SEVEN STOP THEN IN A LINE AUGUST EIGHTY-SEVEN MARCH EIGHTY-EIGHT DECEMBER EIGHTY-EIGHT APRIL THIS YEAR STOP FIRST TIME MURDER THEN ARMED ROBBERY STOP MURDER STOP MURDER STOP WANTED IN TEXAS NEW MEXICO COLORADO KANSAS STOP ANYTHING ELSE STOP SHANE.

Kane folded the telegram, paid and mounted again. He headed south towards Pampa where Caine was waiting.

Well, Kane thought, so the reward was increased three times while Whittaker was there in the village. Either Whittaker had angels' wings which could bring him from Texas to Colorado in one night or the man who had done these crimes was somebody else.

Kane had no doubts about what the answer was.

But only Caine could prove it.

Chapter 11

Peter Caine sat on the plank verandah outside the hotel when Kane came riding up. The gang leader had – in spite of the intense warmth – a thick woollen suit on and on his head he wore a round, stiff hat with a narrow brim.

He should have looked ridiculous, Kane thought as he dismounted and tied his horse outside the hotel. Caine didn't smile or wave. He just sat still staring at Kane.

Kane removed his hat and dusted his trousers with it. A grey cloud of dust blew away slowly.

'You're early,' Caine said slowly.

Kane put on his hat and looked at him. He felt pressure building up inside him. He made sure his voice didn't show any signs of his mood.

'Didn't take so long,' he answered.

'Fetch the reward?'

'No.'

Caine raised his eyebrows. 'Oh?'

Kane said coldly, 'If you had told me what kind of person this Whittaker was I'd never have gone after him in the village.'

'And what kind of person was he, Marlow?'

'A sadist. The inhabitants in the village tore him apart with their bare hands.'

'Why didn't you try and stop it?' Caine's voice was hard, feelingless.

'I didn't give a shit,' Kane said, challengingly. 'Just a pity he was dead when they did it.'

Caine's face paled with anger. 'Your softness cost us eight thousand dollars, Marlow.' And then came the rest, almost without a pause, 'Why'd you ride into Amarillo on the way north?'

Kane felt the pressure increasing. He knew that in a few seconds he was going to lose control – and draw.

He said, 'That's none of your damned business, Caine.'

Time seemed to stand still a few seconds. Kane could feel the beat of his heart right down in his fingertips. Now! he thought. Now! But he just stood there. Only the lines around his mouth and the narrowed, glittering eyes showed anything.

Caine said slowly and carefully, 'We've depended on you, Marlow. We gave you the fattest bait in the district. You just dropped a small fortune. And you rode into Amarillo. I'll ask again – why?'

Kane felt rather than saw Tom Conway was placed in one of the rooms that had its window out towards the street. Maybe he was sighting on Kane right now behind one of the curtains. Caine's calmness was proof of it. Kane relaxed. He managed to smile – a pretence of a smile.

'A bad habit. Just have to have me a woman before a fight. It calms the nerves. And maybe it'll always be the last time.'

Caine stared still. Something in his expression told Kane that he had answered correctly.

'All right.' The short answer proved that he had been followed and watched carefully in Amarillo. He just hoped that his shadow hadn't been into the house on Hobart Street and had been told of his night trip.

'Back to Whittaker,' Caine went on. 'Why didn't you lure him out of town?'

The question came so easy that Kane almost blurted out the fact that Whittaker hadn't left the village for almost two years – even though his reward continued to rise . . . If Kane *had* mentioned it it would have told Caine that the swindle had been exposed. Should he play dumb? Or . . .

Kane said, 'You know damned well that Whittaker's price was two thousand before you started to pump it up. If it's idiots you need, Caine, then I'm not the man.' He made a move – as if he was about to go.

'Hold it!'

Through the shout Kane heard the click of a rifle hammer

being drawn back. Sweat started to run down his back. He half turned towards Caine.

'Don't push me too far,' he sneered. 'I don't like being pushed around or fooled. So let's just forget the whole thing, eh? Adios, Caine.'

'I'm sorry about this, Marlow,' the gang leader said behind him, and Kane stopped, uncertain of what to do. 'Come back here and let's have a drink. I shouldn't have underestimated you.'

Kane made out he was considering it. Inside he was weak with relief. His bluff had worked, beyond all expectations.

'I like open cards between us,' he said coldly.

Caine rose. 'Let's go inside.'

Kane was told the whole story – briefly. But it was enough to fill in the gaps, enough to send Conway, Caine and a good many others to the gallows. It was a simple method really. It was done by using three principles, the first was to get their hands on a man who was wanted and had a price on his head, get him out of circulation and then make sure he got the blame for other things too, so that the price was raised after a while. Caine then chose a man who was about the same size as the wanted man, dressed him the same way, same weapons, same habits, made him as similar as possible. Even the voice was copied and the tactics used again and again, usually by leaving some kind of 'proof' at the scene of the crime. It didn't always work but when it did the trouble was well worth it.

The other method was to capture a criminal and force him to join them on robberies, making sure that he was seen all the time. This was pretty difficult but they were sure of doubling the price when it did work. The third was to wait until the criminal himself had raised the price on his own head and then kill him, for the reward. Whittaker fitted number two of these methods. Caine made sure that each of the crimes was performed with Whittaker's merciless brutality, usually crowning it with rape. The man who performed these deeds was unbelievably like Whittaker in looks and a number of witnesses swore that they had seen him when they were shown the description of him.

Caine leaned back in his chair and sipped from his glass. 'You understand – I *make*, create the situations, Marlow – I don't sit around just waiting for them to happen. It's amazing the way a little boot blacking in the hair, wax in the cheeks and some padding in the clothing can change a person so much. Whittaker was tall, blond, gangling. There were a lot of tall, blond crooks in Texas but Whittaker had the lobe of his left ear missing – an important detail. And five hundred dollars . . . isn't that good pay for the loss of an ear lobe? Whittaker's "twin" thought so – and my investments paid off . . . six thousand dollars.'

Tom Conway picked his teeth with a thin-bladed knife. Kane noticed that he pushed it into the top of his right boot when he was finished. He said, 'Don't think this happens often, Marlow. Eighty per cent of them are just crooks with a first reward hanging over them. It's simple, sure and without risk then.'

The way Conway said this – and his glance at Caine – told Kane that Conway wasn't completely in agreement with the big chances his boss took.

Caine smiled mockingly, 'Tom only believes in certainties. What do you think, Marlow?'

'If it can be combined, then okay, I reckon.'

Caine sipped his beer. 'Shame it went wrong, the Whittaker business,' he said. 'But let's forget it. Willing to try again?'

Kane squinted at him through the smoke. 'If you take the chance I'm more than willing.' He let his eagerness show through, the eagerness to make good again, give a better picture of himself, deserve the gang's thanks and admiration for a job well done . . .

'All right. We've got a contact in Dumas.' The smile was on Kane who returned it. 'This contact,' Caine went on, 'has discovered a man who started a small business, a gun shop. Our man thought there was something about this man he recognised so he started snooping around. Sure, he was wanted for train robbery in the best Jesse James style, wanted in Alabama and Mississippi. He got away with over forty thousand dollars. This happened about two years ago. The price is ten per cent – four thousand. So if you feel like a trip north, he's all yours, Marlow. As compensation for Whittaker I'll go fifty-fifty with you. Okay?'

Kane raised his glass and looked at the golden whisky. His grey eyes had a hard, cold gleam.

'Okay,' he said, 'it'll be a pleasure.'

Kane rode north the following morning. At the first telegraph station he reached he stopped and sent a telegram. When he had done it he once again headed for Dumas. Two days later he was there and went straight to the hotel. He signed in, had his baggage sent up and lay down to sleep. A couple of hours later he woke up. After a bath and shave he felt fresh and rested. He loosened the Wayne Martin holster from the belt and placed it in the top of his waist-band. A couple of quick draws and he knew he had adjusted it correctly. Satisfied, he grabbed his hat, shut and locked the door behind him and went downstairs.

In the 'Drifters Bar' he immediately caught sight of the young man in the dark, well-fitting suit who stood over by the bar and played with some dice. He looked at Kane without any sign of recognition. Kane took a drink, bought half a bottle and went over to an empty table. As he passed he mumbled a couple of words to the young man.

Kane left the bar about eleven o'clock and went back to the hotel. He bought a new bottle from the man in the reception and took it up with him. He drew the curtains, pulled up two chairs to the table and filled a glass. Then he sat in one of the chairs and began to play with a pack of cards.

Twenty minutes later the door was knocked just once then a nail scraped the door. Kane said, 'Come in.'

Marshal Hank Vernon came in and shut the door quietly behind him.

'Take a drink,' Kane said after shaking hands with him. Vernon sat down and poured himself a glass.

'I jumped on the first train,' he said. His greyish-blue eyes showed a certain excitement. And this was the case. Kane was to Vernon – like many other young marshals – very special, a man who always experienced the most unbelievable things, a man who attracted trouble and drama and beautiful women in a strange way. It was the second time he was going to work together with Kane and Vernon's thoughts went back to the day when he, Kane and a handful of others stormed Bravado's headquarters and killed the whole gang and then Kane had almost lost his life when Bravado blew himself and the girl in the mausoleum to pieces.

Almost like thought-reading Kane's thoughts went back to the same incident. The young man reminded him of the day that *she* had died. He dropped the thoughts. He concentrated on Vernon. He had asked Shane to send Vernon. The young man was – after himself – the corps' best man with a gun. Kane knew that Tom Conway and Peter Caine were too many for one man. He hadn't felt in the least embarrassed when he admitted that he needed help. Kane had grown beyond all forms of false pride.

He could see excitement, admiration and respect in the young blue in front of him. Kane suddenly felt sick. He thought of Conway's sudden burst of laughter. Would that be the last sound Vernon ever heard? He pushed the thought away and said, 'I've got a new gun-job for you, Hank. Are you in condition? Real fine form?'

Vernon never flinched. 'Sure.'

'The name Tom Conway mean anything to you?'

'No.'

Kane sipped his liquor. He wanted to get rid of that admiring gleam in Vernon's eyes, he wanted him to be aware, to listen.

'I've seen him and I think he's as fast as you are. This is something a little more than blowing shit out of paper cards.'

'I'm aware of that.' Vernon's eyes were sharp now and a slight blush appeared on his cheeks. Kane saw it and went on, 'There's one for each of us, Hank. Mine's called Peter Caine.'

Vernon looked at Kane. He didn't get it. Why was Kane on edge? Conway and Caine. The names meant nothing to him.

He looked into Kane's eyes. His throat dried up. There was something nasty about Kane. Something . . . something that made him feel like . . . feel like . . . like what? Oh, shit!

Kane quickly explained about the organisation and everything he knew, mentioning a few names that Vernon memorised and then finally he told him about Whittaker.

'They gave me another chance,' Kane said. 'A guy who's settled here in town and owns a gun shop in Dumas. He's worth four thousand and I'm to fetch the reward.'

Vernon looked at his cigarette. He said nothing.

'When I've got the reward I ride back to Pampa with the

money. You follow me – at a distance. I don't reckon on being watched but be careful just in case. Maybe I'll get another job straight away, I don't know. But I want you to drop in on Pampa just after I arrive. You're a cow-hand, flat broke and you take a room you can just about afford – let's say one dollar a night. Stay out of circulation but keep your eyes open. The gang stays at the hotel. There's only one in town so you can't make a mistake. I don't know if there are more than just Conway and Caine there. Best to say that there are others. In some way or another I'll contact you there. That's all.'

Vernon got up without emptying his glass. His eyes were as hard as flint.

'You planning on killing this guy in the store?'

'You bet your life I am,' Kane said brutally. *'I'm killing for the law.'*

Vernon didn't answer, grabbed his hat and quietly shut the door behind him.

Kane sat a while deep in thought. He wondered if he had gone too far. No, he didn't think so. Vernon was an ace on the range at Alvarado, a man who attracted a crowd when he practised. He used a gun as if he was in a circus act. Kane didn't like it. Not that he didn't think the young man was good enough, but it did no harm to get him a bit angry, a bit on edge. It sharpened his instincts. It was one thing to shoot at a card, a target, but it was another matter to meet a gunman face to face in a gunfight.

He sighed and corked the bottle. He undressed, blew out the lamp and lay down.

The following morning he ate breakfast in the hotel and then went out. He found the gunshop on the edge of town, in a street where there was also a bakery, a smithy, and a stable. The shop was in one wing of a new building. In the window were three or four revolvers and some carbines behind a steel grill.

Kane opened the door. A bell rang above his head. The room was small. It was divided in two by a counter. The wall behind the counter was covered in glass cases and racks. A glance through a door to the back room showed the back of a man in working clothes and wearing a leather apron. He was bent over a vice.

'Just a moment, mister,' he shouted without turning.

'No hurry,' Kane answered. He glanced out of the door. The street was empty. He looked around. A number of good rifles on racks. Behind the glass doors revolvers flashed dully in the light.

The filing sound stopped and a stool creaked. A man in his forties appeared. He was wiping his hands on an oily cloth. His face was broad, strong, and his hair was thinning.

'What can I do for you, mister?'

Kane drew his revolver slowly from his holster. 'I wondered if you'd take a look at this, Mr Kells.'

The man looked startled. 'Kells?' he said, trying to force a laugh. He pointed towards the door. 'The name's Howard, mister.'

Kane still held the revolver in his hand. 'Your name is Kells and you're from Georgia,' he said slowly. 'Two years ago you robbed the Vicksburg lines of a great deal of cash, getting away with forty thousand dollars. You're worth four thousand . . . dead or alive.'

Kane cocked the hammer of his gun.

Kells was pale now. Pearls of sweat trickled down his face.

'Don't shoot, mister! God, this must be a mistake! I'm called Howard, I can prove it!'

'I've seen the poster with your picture on it, Mr Kells. It's all over now, curtains for you, Kells.'

Kells glared at the black hole in Kane's Colt, paralysed with fear. His Adam's apple rose up and down like a piston.

'Don't shoot . . . for God's sake!' he gasped. 'That's right, I'm Kells, but I've still got most of the cash and can get away with just a few years inside! Don't shoot, mister . . . you'll get your four thousand anyway . . . and I can add . . . ten thousand! How about it?'

Kane pushed his left hand down into the left boot. When he pulled up his hand the marshal star shone in it.

'Relax, Kells,' he said. 'I won't shoot. Get rid of that apron. We're goin' down to the sheriff's office.'

Ten minutes later Sheriff Orville Bate locked the door of the cell behind Kells and chuckled at Kane.

'Well, who gets the cash. You?'

'No. I can't accept it.'

'Oh, just bait, eh?'

Kane had been forced to tell the sheriff some of the story. He *had* to have four thousand to show in Pampa.

The sheriff wrote out a note to the bank, the Amarillo Trust Bank, and handed it to Kane. Kane pushed it in his pocket. He intended to draw out the cash the same day and ride back to Pampa as fast as possible. The proof was there now. The last act was about to take place.

Kane nodded to the sheriff and left. He took the money in hundred dollar bills and went back to the hotel. On the way he passed Vernon. They didn't even look at each other. Vernon no longer wore the smart suit. He was dressed in a sweat-stained denim outfit with a worn, calf-skin vest. His hat looked battered out of all recognition.

He certainly looked like a flat-broke, out-of-work cow-hand.

Chapter 12

For the third time in succession Kane passed the wind-swept churchyard up on the hill and rode slowly down to Pampa. It had clouded over and was humid, and far away it thundered somewhere. It sounded like a herd of buffalo on the move.

Kane's face was grey with dust. He pulled the bandana from his nose and mouth and spat dryly. It had been a hard trip and the horse was just about all in.

He caught sight of Peter Caine in the basket chair outside the hotel. Kane suddenly had the urge to whip out the carbine and gun him down there and then. But he fought the desire when he saw the watchful eyes under the ridiculous hat. Caine wore his thick jacket but this time he had undone it and Kane could see the black single revolver belt that hung around the strong hips. His thoughts went to the unique weapon that hung in the belt's holster and his mouth was dry at the thought of the hollow click the hammer had made on an empty chamber up in the hotel room.

'Welcome, Marlow,' Caine said casually. 'Everything okay?'

'Went like a dream. Just walked him down to the sheriff. Went as peaceful as a lamb. Thought it best not to shoot. Maybe we'll get another chance at him again, who knows.' As he talked Kane felt an instinctive unease. He knew that he couldn't ignore it. His eyes narrowed. He stared at Caine. Was that a secret smile on the thick lips? Was there an unnatural quietness in the streets? Was it *too* quiet in the hotel? And where was Conway? Had he reason to stand guard in a window now?

His throat was even drier now.

'Got the money, Marlow?'

Was that a slight pause before Caine had said Marlow? Was this the cat playing with the mouse? Kane felt a shudder of fear go through him. Had the real Marlow got away? Had Waldron got a message to them? Was Caine aware that he was talking to a U.S. marshal right now? The silver star seemed to burn in his boot. Had they discovered it when they searched him? No, impossible! The seam hadn't moved a fraction. What was it then? Just nerves?

He dismounted – slowly and stiffly as if he was aching all over and tired. He loosened the saddle bag. The revolver holster, which was now on his belt again, was shoved over half an inch. Kane noticed it. 'Money's here.' He dropped the bag on to the planks. 'I'm as thirsty as a coyote.'

Caine smiled. 'We'd better do something about it. Come in and get yourself a drink.'

Kane stared at the broad back as Caine walked quite naturally in first. Imagination, he said to himself.

It wasn't until he entered the semi-darkness of the hallway that he realised it wasn't imagination. Out of the corner of his eye – on the edge of his range of vision – a shadow was flashing towards his head. The heavy stick caught the side of his head, his fingers loosened around the revolver and he fell flat on his face . . .

A glowing sun hung above him. It was white – enormous. It covered his range of vision. He could feel its heat. He could smell burned hair where his eyebrows and eyelashes were smouldering.

Then the sun began to diminish as it revolved. Kane felt sick with the wild rotating. He tried to shut his eyes but they wouldn't shut. The sun was just a piercing speck now. Now it broke into two. The specks became two eyes.

They were staring at him.

'He's coming round,' a voice said.

Kane lay on his back. His feet were tied to the legs at the foot of an iron bed. His arms were tied round the bed posts by his head. He was spread-eagled across the bed. His whole body ached with the pressure of the rope around his joints.

His eyes began to focus. Tom Conway stood beside the bed.

Peter Caine sat in an armchair beside him. On the other side stood two men, dark-skinned and wearing faded cotton shirts and canvas trousers. They looked stupid, like two morons.

Kane looked around. He lay in his own room. All right, he thought, this is the end of the road. His fighting spirit reacted immediately to the feeling of defeat. He sneered: 'What the hell's the meaning of this? Aren't you lot getting tired of this?'

Caine turned his head. He said mildly, 'You are a brilliant actor, Mr Kane. Just a pity that there is no audience to listen to you this time.'

It hit Kane like a blow. His mind reeled with 'hows' and 'whys'.

'What the hell are you gabbling about, Caine?' he said angrily. 'And who the hell's this "Kane" you're talking about?'

'Kane is a U.S. marshal,' Caine said slowly, but his eyes had an insane gleam in them now. 'He is known to be an adventurer. But the adventure is over now, Mr Marshal!'

Caine drew his revolver slowly, with almost loving movements. Just as slowly he released the catch and flipped open the cylinder. One after another he flipped out the cartridges until there were nine shining in his hand.

Kane started to sweat.

Caine carefully chose one bullet and placed it in the cylinder. Then he locked it.

He smiled at Kane. With his thumb he drew back the hammer a fraction, to release the lock, and let the cylinder rotate with a soft ticking sound. The rotation stopped and Caine raised the octagonal barrel up towards his nose and waved it to and fro.

'Have you heard of "Russian Roulette", Kane? Surely you have. Briefly it is when you load a pistol with one cartridge, let the cylinder spin and then cock it. With a normal revolver there is one chance in six that there is a bullet lying beneath the firing pin. Some men have earned fortunes at this game, but it does happen sometimes that they make a mistake.'

He smiled and pressed harder on the revolver against his nose. His nose was pressed upwards. Kane looked straight into the black hairy nostrils. He felt nauseated.

Caine aimed at a point between Kane's eyes. He continued to talk while his knuckles grew white around the trigger.

'I must admit that I was fooled by you, Kane. It is with regret that I admit it. You are the first man who has managed to do that. But I was beginning to get suspicious. Waldron should have shown up. He is quite a man for the women . . . but . . . not *that* much.'

Kane stared into the revolver barrel. Was there a bullet beneath the hammer now? His heart was beating like a piston rod in his chest.

'The other thing was that "Marlow" had too much money on him. A hunter can himself be hunted at any time – and thirty thousand or more was too much to run around with.'

While he talked, Caine's trigger finger was pressing harder and harder on the trigger. The trigger spring must be just about . . .

The click sounded like thunder in Kane's ears.

'First round to you, Mr Kane!' Caine said. 'But, to continue. When I was too suspicious I arranged this last trip. A few hours before you came I got this telegram from our man in Amarillo.'

He cocked the pistol again. Sweat ran down into Kane's eyes. The cylinder had flipped one place to the right. Was the bullet under the firing pin *now*? Or had it been in position when the cylinder first stopped spinning and had it been pushed round with the first cocking of the hammer, having to go all round before arriving beneath the firing pin again?

'Read the telegram, Tom,' Caine said. His finger started to squeeze again. Kane's muscles reacted instinctively and he pulled at the ropes, cursing and swearing with distorted lips.

'MARLOW IS A FAKE. THE NAME IS KANE. U.S. MARSHAL. WATCH OUT. Signed B.'

'B., Mr Kane. Bate, Sheriff Bate. Do you now understand why we are so well informed?'

Kane's face stiffened in a horrible grimace when he realised that it was just before it happened. He tensed his muscles against it . . .

Click.

'You are unusually lucky, Mr Kane,' the gangleader went on. 'But the odds have changed now. A mathematician could tell you that after two empty shots from a nine shot cylinder with one chamber loaded, the chances have fallen to exactly ninety per cent.'

A muffled click and the hammer was cocked for the third time. Suddenly Kane's fear and anger disappeared, and he no longer felt helpless. He felt it, and knew why.

The bullet was now in place under the firing pin! He didn't know why, he just knew that it was true. Perhaps a person who is about to die feels these things, he thought.

His body relaxed. He wouldn't feel any pain; he would be aware, perhaps, of the flash, feel the pressure of the gas in his face – then it would be over.

Kane's heart calmed down. Resigned – like a wounded animal – he waited for death.

Hank Vernon was cold with anger when he left Kane's room and came out on to the street. Kane didn't have to behave like that, even though being the older one he gave the orders. Then he thought – after all, it was *him* that Kane wanted – not Zachary, not Meyer, not Fitzgerald, none of the older, more experienced marshals. Vernon stopped on the sidewalk, deep in thought. He thought of Kane's face as he remembered it from the fight with Bravado's gang – it had been just as cold, brutal, merciless. It had spread to all of them. They had dived into the fight as one man, and they had cleared the floor easily. Was this just a tactic from Kane to sharpen the senses and prepare him against the coming battle? Vernon hurried through the dark streets in Dumas. It was *he* whom Kane had chosen! Vernon swore an oath to himself on the way back to the hotel. He would rather die than let Kane down, now that he had shown his trust.

He followed Kane on the long trip south, keeping a safe distance. The worn clothing he had obtained suited him well. Vernon wasn't used to wearing suits and lace ties. Not so many years before, worn clothing like this was all he had owned, that was when he sweated as a town marshal for fifty dollars a month and his keep. Vernon had received his baptism of fire in a ranch war, when half a dozen hired guns on each side turned the fight into something more than a neighbourly squabble. He emerged from the battle with his life and three deadly draws that his right hand had made. The long hours behind the barn practising with his revolver had paid dividends. He had a reputation suddenly and started to roam, drift about like other young men with fire in their blood and lightning in their gun hands. There was a fifty-fifty chance that he would end his days as a wanted killer after some bar-room fight. Vernon didn't avoid fights and always killed his opponents. Among the interested observers was a man whose brother was a U.S. marshal. He mentioned the young man to his brother. That was the start.

Vernon had been in the corps for three years and he still wasn't thirty years old. If he wasn't killed he had all the makings of a brilliant career ahead of him.

Vernon pulled the hat down over his forehead and kept his eyes on the almost invisible dust cloud ahead. An unpractised eye would think it to be a whirlwind . . . clouds of dust whipped up into the air. But Vernon had grown up in South Dakota and had all his life known the difference between the two. It had been a necessity where he had come from. Dust was the only warning the pioneers were given before the Kiowa Indians were on top of them.

The landscape – with North Canada in the west and the Prairie to the south – reminded him of Dakota. It was just as dry, wind-swept and naked. Range of vision was just as hazy, wind just as hot, smell of dust the same. Vernon hated this country, as he hated Dakota and the Kiowa territory.

While he sat rocking in the saddle on the road south, he thought of the day almost ten years before when he had ridden south following tracks – tracks from a band of Kiowa. He remembered the place where the Indians had left his father, dead, mutilated. He remembered that the Indians had stuck sharp sticks in his father's head. Even though his father was dead, the sight of the sticks protruding out of his head had shocked him more than the gaping wounds from their tomahawks. Later he was told that the Kiowa used these sticks on the dead enemies they respected. The meaning was to entice out the dead man's brave soul.

Indians are strange like that, Vernon reflected, as he rode, keeping his eyes on the wind and dust. I remember the first time I saw people that the Arapaho had left behind. I was warned, but was too curious. Okay – I spewed, but at least I saw that the eyes of the dead had been poked out and placed by the feet of the corpses. At first I couldn't understand why. I remember thinking the scout was lying when he said that the eyes were there so that they could *see* the humiliation of the dead.

He rolled a cigarette and lit it. I'm glad the Indian wars are almost over, he thought. I've done a lot of things but I've never been as afraid as I was when fighting the Indians. They aren't like us whites. Look at the Apaches. When a boy is fourteen he has to go through a test of manhood, he's not allowed to fight or steal horses or anything like that – no, they just give him a mouthful of water and let him run through a desert hell, and when he comes out he's got to spit out the water . . .

The sun shone in the sky. A couple of buzzards hung like two specks against the hazy blue sky. Vernon glanced up at them with stinging eyes. He hated buzzards. New thoughts of his boyhood came to mind. He smoked and let the memories come. Time passed quicker this way. Vernon passed the churchyard on Boot Hill, Pampa, exactly as Kane turned the corner down in the main street and caught sight of Caine on the verandah.

Vernon turned and came into town from the north. He was dusty and filthy and his horse didn't look much better. He let the horse move at its own pace, but his eyes were glancing to and fro beneath the brim of his hat. By a stroke of luck he crossed the main street where the hotel was and found himself looking straight down at the hotel façade. Vernon remembered that Kane had mentioned this hotel and he cursed himself for not noticing the building at once. He stared at the hotel. Suddenly he felt his throat dry up. He saw Kane standing with his face turned towards the hotel verandah and talk to a man in dark clothing who sat in the basket chair there. Vernon let the horse back up a few paces into the shadow of the alley way. He was about a hundred yards away but could easily make out Kane. The men talked for a few minutes. Then the man in the chair got up and went in first. Kane followed him.

Simple, peaceful, Vernon thought and wondered how he was going to ask for a room. He glanced at the hotel windows.

Then he saw it, clearly. The sun reflecting off something metallic. Somebody had moved away from the window. Had he been watching Kane? Had Kane walked into a trap? Or was it just a security measure?

Vernon swung down from his horse and led it towards the hotel. He had to keep a poker face now. He threw the reins loosely around the hitching post in front of the hotel and brushed the dust off himself. He walked across the splintered verandah floor and into the shadow of the doorway. Through the semi-darkness he could make out the counter, an open guest book, a brass bell and a dirty quill pen. He said, 'Hey, anybody here?'

A door opened behind the counter. A man in dirty cotton clothes appeared. He looked the filthy bum up and down a few times.

'What d'ya want?'

'A room, mister . . . if it ain't too costly.'

Vernon spoke with a drawling Tennessee accent. Was that an uneasy look in the man's eyes?

'Cheapest costs eight dollars.'

Vernon sighed. 'Too much for me. Okay . . . guess I'll just have to sleep out tonight. Thanks, mister.'

On the way out his eyes noticed small details. There were two small piles of dust on the floor. And a few minute flecks of blood that hadn't dried into the boards yet. Together the piles of dust and blood flecks formed a triangle. A picture of a prone man flashed through Vernon's mind, blood from the head, dust from each boot.

He was sure that Kane had been knocked down, maybe killed. He had to get into the hotel somehow . . .

Vernon whistled cheerfully as he loosened the reins and climbed into the saddle. He felt eyes on his back as he moved off and rode down the street. Then he turned the first corner. Now he moved with lightning speed. He forced the horse into a narrow side street and tied it up. Crouching, he ran past two plank fences and a pile of rubbish that lay in the hotel back-yard. It still wasn't two minutes since he left the hotel. He sneaked quickly along the fence and up to the half open door. He reckoned on it leading to a store room or maybe kitchen. The smell of food told him it was the kitchen. Vernon drew his Colt and pushed open the door. A narrow, dirty corridor. The smell of beans and bacon was sickening. He passed two open doors. He heard voices and the sound of kitchen equipment.

The inner door was shut. He tried to open it. The door wasn't locked.

With a push he sent it swinging inwards. The man in white who had spoken to him in the lobby whirled around. His hand flashed down towards a gun in the open drawer. Vernon dived forward. The heavy revolver barrel was smashed down on the man's head. He dropped out of the chair. Vernon grabbed him and let him fall to the floor quietly. He listened. Somewhere in the house he could hear the mumble of voices. He was in a room just behind the lobby. He glanced out and was facing the open door to the street. His eyes settled on a sign leaning up against the wall, 'Back soon'. Vernon laughed and placed it on the counter. Then he dodged out into the lobby, shut the door behind him and fled up the stairs to the second floor. He crept down the corridor and listened. Somewhere he could hear a man snoring. He went on. Now he could hear voices. He put his ear against the door.

' . . . a mathematician could tell you that after two empty shots from a nine shot cylinder with one chamber loaded, the chances have fallen to ninety per cent.'

Vernon felt his nerves tighten. What in hell was that guy on about? Russian Roulette? Then it came!

'You are afraid, Mr Kane? I think you have reason to be . . . !'

Vernon didn't waste a second. He gripped his revolver tightly and threw himself against the thin door.

There was a crash as the shadowy figure burst into the room. Everything happened within three seconds.

All four men whirled around as Vernon came rushing in. Caine's finger had been on the point of pulling the trigger and he instinctively pointed the gun at the marshal. The bullet – the one which would have splintered Kane's head – smashed into the wall just above Vernon's head. The young marshal fired before he hit the floor. He fired two shots at Tom Conway because he was the best and clearest target, one towards Caine who had started to rise from the chair and one at each of the two helpers dressed in white. Vernon fired with a speed and precision that would have sent the firing instructor into an ecstasy. As he fired at Conway he saw Conway draw with incredible speed. Vernon's first shot tore through his left shoulder.

The other grazed his throat, severing the main artery. When Caine realised that he had missed with his only shot he was on the way out of the chair. At the same time Vernon swung his gun at him. It most likely saved Caine's life. Vernon's bullet smashed straight through Caine's right shoulder so the padding flew up in the air. Caine fell backwards towards the window. The two men in white hadn't a chance. Before their revolvers were half-way out of their holsters Vernon stopped them. Lying on his stomach with both hands around his revolver he shot first the one, then the other exactly between the eyes.

Then everything was suddenly deafeningly, thunderingly still. Vernon was pale and trembling when he got to his feet and saw Kane's spreadeagled body lying across the bed. Tom Conway was screaming. Vernon suddenly realised that he had been doing so all the time. Blood was gushing out of the mortal wound in his throat. Vernon got a mouthful of bile as he grabbed a revolver on the floor and shot Conway through the heart.

'Get these ropes off me,' Kane said hoarsely.

Vernon had to fight to get the knife out, his hands trembled so much. It smelled sickening, terrible in the overheated room.

As Vernon bent over Kane, Caine rose from the floor and a knife was suddenly protruding from Vernon's back, and as Kane heard the young man's scream of pain, he saw Caine's huge body smash the window in a desperate dive and disappear outside.

With a jerk Kane snapped the half-severed ropes and sprang to the window. He just caught a glimpse of the darkly dressed figure on a horse as he turned a corner and disappeared.

Kane swore in hatred. Vernon lay on his stomach across the bed. The knife shaft moved with each gasp of breath he made. It rattled deep in the young man's throat.

Kane sprang over to him. To hell with Caine now!

He bent over the boy. The knife sat deep, fairly high up on the right hand side. As long as it hadn't touched the lungs . . . !

He said quietly, 'You hear me, Hank?'

Vernon turned his head. 'Yeah,' he moaned. 'Christ, Kane . . . get it out . . .'

Kane clenched his teeth and grabbed the hilt. The knife was stuck as if it was in wood.

He pulled. Vernon screamed – one long, terrible scream – then he relaxed and passed out.

Blood gushed over Kane's hands. He grabbed a sheet, tore it into strips and made a large, hard compress. The bleeding stopped. Kane was breathing heavily as he bandaged the young man. The thought that Vernon should die on his hands was too terrible to think of.

Wood creaked. Kane dived to one side as he registered the sound. While he was still moving he snatched at a revolver that lay on the floor, in the middle of a pool of blood. A shot roared. Blood and splinters exploded around him. Kane's slippery fingers gripped the revolver. A figure dressed in white filled the doorway. Kane fired three times, so fast the shots sounded as one. The figure was flung backwards and hit the floor with a crash. Kane climbed to his feet and wiped the blood off his hands. Then he caught sight of his own revolver in the corner. As he buckled the belt on he heard shouts and footsteps from the street. He went over to the window and glanced out, expecting a shot to come. A group of men and women stood there staring up at him. None of them bore weapons. Kane took a desperate chance, fished the star out and stood in the window. He held his star towards them and started to talk, fast, loudly.

Chapter 13

He found the tracks at the water hole by White Deer, about seventy kilometres north of Pampa. Caine obviously had little time, he had only stopped to let his horse drink.

Kane followed the tracks northwards. It amazed him that Caine didn't take a more westerly course – towards Dumas, for example. But Caine was no fool and was certain that Kane would inform the authorities about Sheriff Bate in Dumas as quickly as possible. And Kane had done just that. It turned out that nobody in town knew about the business Caine dealt in. To them he was just a rich eccentric. They had carried Vernon down and an old, drunken doctor had sworn that the young man would survive – and not only that but he'd be on his feet again in four weeks' time. Kane had got the mayor to act as marshal until the authorities cleared up the case, and the fat, sweating mayor had been ridiculously solemn as Kane swore him in. The new marshal promised to send the long telegram Kane had written and Kane went after Caine feeling more assured now. He wondered if Caine was aware that he was being followed. He should be. Kane decided to reckon on the gang leader knowing he was being followed.

He followed the tracks until it grew dark. There he made a simple bed in some bushes and at the first rays of dawn was in the saddle again. The tracks pointed steadily north – towards Dodge City. Was that where Caine was heading? Or was it just that he intended to swing around Dodge and go on, on through Kansas to Nebraska, Wyoming or South Dakota? The distances were enormous and Kane knew it. He pushed his horse until it was stumbling and then a little more. Slowly but surely he cut down the lead that Caine had. When they were a day's ride from Dodge the tracks were not more than a couple of hours old. They pointed towards the broad valley where the town lay. Kane had no doubts any longer. Caine was heading for Dodge. Just a coincidence? Kane wondered. It had been in Dodge that he had first got on the gang's trail. His thoughts went to Peggy Lamar. She had been the start. Caine couldn't be . . . or could he? Something cold and painful gripped Kane's chest. Was Caine going mad? Did he think that Waldron in a drunken fit had balled about everything? Did he think that Kane had learned about the gang from *her*? Was this a last act of revenge? Kane didn't wait for an answer. He spurred the horse into a gallop. The valley opened before him. How long could the horse keep this speed up? One hour . . . two? How strong was Caine's horse?

Kane rode like a machine. He used his fists and spurs mercilessly. Foam flew off the stallion's flanks. Kane hated to treat a horse like this but he had no choice now. When the tracks went around a stretch with sand and boulders Kane forced the horse out into the stony stretch. He could make up a few hours here – or lose if the horse broke a leg.

It worked. Kane got through. But he noticed that the horse's movements were getting stiffer and stiffer. A terrible rumbling in the animal's chest told him that it was nearing the end of its tether. He could see the smoke from town now. Just a mile or so away. A mist of exhaustion and tiredness lay across his eyes. He just wanted to stop and give up. But he forced the animal on. The horse's breathing was now just a rattle. Suddenly he caught sight of Caine. His horse was just trotting along. It's head was bowed, exhausted, and Caine was swaying in the saddle. How far away was he? Five hundred yards? Could he reach Caine with his rifle? No, not a chance.

His horse stumbled and went down on one knee. Kane dragged it up and made it go on. Then it stumbled again. The horse fell heavily and Kane had to dive out of the saddle to avoid being crushed beneath it. He swore in anger and desperation. Caine was just a few hundred yards away now from the nearest house. A dog began to bark there. A cow bellowed some way away.

Kane started to run. There was Caine now, disappearing between the buildings. He ran and ran, stumbled, slipped, fell – struggled up and ran on. The blood was hammering in his temples now . . . he could taste bile in his mouth.

On, Kane, on . . . on!

He passed the first buildings. Where was Caine? Gone. Where was her house? Which street? Somebody stopped and looked at him in fear. Kane ran on, deathly pale, his face distorted. He caught sight of a huge, dark back in the street. Kane was given an extra spurt of energy. He stumbled on, stumbled, lost his hat, couldn't be bothered to try and pick it up. Caine turned down a side street. The low evening sun threw a long shadow on the wall of a house in front of him. How far away was he now? Fifty yards? But Peggy's house was just around the corner! Kane remembered the little, quiet street with the poplars. Sweat burned his eyes. He rubbed his face as he ran.

As he swung around the corner into *her* street Caine stopped and looked back. Maybe he felt that he was being followed, maybe he heard Kane's gasping breath and stumbling steps.

Caine stopped.

Kane stopped too.

There was thirty yards between them. They stood there, feet apart, trembling with exhaustion, gasping for breath. The same thought came to each of them – you're too tired and weak to draw and shoot now!

Kane's lungs were almost bursting. It was as if he had knives under each shoulder blade. His legs shook under him. He could only just stand.

Caine wasn't breathing so hard, but he was weak from loss of blood. His left jacket sleeve was black with dried blood from Vernon's bullet. His left hand was also covered in blood. His eyes were wide open, staring, as if he couldn't believe what he saw. Seconds passed. The sun sank slowly lower. The shadow from a tall poplar crept towards Caine.

Kane stood there, feeling just as terrible and weak. If Caine drew now he was done for. He knew it. He just couldn't be bothered to draw now. The effort would be too much.

A window opened nearby. A woman's voice said something or other. Then she laughed.

Kane's eyes were suddenly deep, glittering. The apathy slipped away, his body gathered its last resources. If he gave up now, Peggy would die. Vernon would maybe die, and for nothing.

That couldn't happen!

All Kane felt as his strength returned was a wild, triumphant joy. He felt his lungs steadying, his heart beating almost normally, feelings in his finger tips, the excitement before the last, lightning draw – even the explosion – began to increase with irresistible power.

'Kane! You shouldn't have followed me here! You hear me? *You shouldn't have followed me here.*'

There had been a touch of hysteria in Caine's voice, fear too! Kane smiled with satanic joy.

'*You're going to die now, Kane!*'

Kane stood there, arms hanging loosely at his sides, his legs apart. His face looked almost black now against the grinning, exposed teeth. His slate grey eyes glittered like crystal.

'*Die Kane!*' Peter Shabarov bellowed and drew his wonderful revolver.

The soft breeze caused the curtains to flap. The chilly morning air crept through the half-open french windows and stroked the silky skin of Peggy Lamar.

She listened to the deep, calm breathing. It was good to hear him sleeping! Peggy shuddered and crept farther down the bed. She knew that she would never forget the sight of him coming staggering up towards the house, bareheaded, his face distorted and sweat pouring down his temples. And the shots . . . the five deafening shots that had frightened the whole neighbourhood. And that huge man who had lain there screaming in a strange language while Kane had stood over him laughing insanely. The people who dared go over there had said that the man on the ground had been shot to pieces. So horrible! And when she asked Kane about this he had said he was an old enemy who had tried to kill him, and that it didn't mean anything and it was better for her to forget the whole thing.

Forget! How could she ever forget that terrible evening and that wonderful night! Peggy Lamar crept up against him. She was filled with warmth when she thought of how ridiculously weak and thankful he had been. How she had helped him out of the filthy, soaked clothing and had washed him like a child. She remembered his weak protests that were drowned in warm water and soap. Then she had sat there, watching him eat, following every mouthful he chewed and swallowed, as women are wont to do, and his wet hair hanging down over his forehead – giving him the appearance of a young, handsome pirate. And later – in front of the flaming open fire – he had taken the first, unbelievable drink that had washed away the last remains of fear and exhaustion. She had seen life return to those grey eyes, seen the gleam in their cold interior, felt his sudden desire for her. Later, in the broad bed, he had woken her own passion, and in each other's arms they had slowly cooled down and slept, embracing each other.

She raised herself on her elbows and looked at his face. In the soft morning light she saw him clearly. She bent nearer to him. Now, while he was asleep and the warmth in his eyes had gone, his face suddenly looked brutal, cold and cynical like a mask. It both attracted and repelled. She lay and looked at him until her elbow hurt. Without taking her eyes off him she pulled a pillow towards her, placed it under her cheek and lay in such a way that she could just lie and look at him until he woke.

THE END

A SELECTION OF FINE READING AVAILABLE IN CORGI BOOKS

Novels

☐	552 08651 7	THE HAND REARED BOY	*Brian W. Aldiss*	35p
☐	552 09018 2	A SOLDIER ERECT	*Brian W. Aldiss*	35p
☐	552 09274 6	A KIND OF LOVING	*Stan Barstow*	40p
☐	552 09277 0	THE DESPERADOES	*Stan Barstow*	30p
☐	552 09278 9	JOBY	*Stan Barstow*	30p
☐	552 09156 1	THE EXORCIST	*William Peter Blatty*	40p
☐	552 07938 3	THE NAKED LUNCH	*William Burroughs*	45p
☐	552 09217 7	THE DWELLING PLACE	*Catherine Cookson*	45p
☐	552 09254 1	MARY ANN'S ANGELS	*Catherine Cookson*	30p
☐	552 09174 X	A CHEMICAL ROMANCE	*Jenny Fabian*	35p
☐	552 09121 9	THE DAY OF THE JACKAL	*Frederick Forsyth*	50p
☐	552 09158 8	THE GOD BENEATH THE SEA	*L. Garfield & E. Blishen*	30p
☐	552 09125 6	CATCH 22	*Joseph Heller*	40p
☐	552 09275 4	SHRINK	*Alec Hilton*	40p
☐	552 09127 8	HOUSE OF LOVE	*Ka-Tzetnik* 135633	35p
☐	552 09019 0	THE CONCUBINE	*Norah Lofts*	35p
☐	552 09256 8	THE LOTUS AND THE WIND	*John Masters*	40p
☐	552 09242 8	WHEN THE DEVIL DRIVES	*Nan Maynard*	35p
☐	552 09240 1	THE DRIFTERS	*James A. Michener*	75p
☐	552 09279 7	STEAMBOAT GOTHIC	*Frances Parkinson Keyes*	50p
☐	552 09140 5	SARAH WHITMAN	*Diane Pearson*	35p
☐	552 09295 9	WE, THE ACCUSED	*Ernest Raymond*	65p
☐	552 09243 6	TELL ENGLAND	*Ernest Raymond*	40p
☐	552 08930 3	STORY OF O	*Pauline Reage*	50p
☐	552 08597 9	PORTNOY'S COMPLAINT	*Philip Roth*	40p
☐	552 08945 1	THE HONEY BADGER	*Robert Ruark*	55p
☐	552 08372 0	LAST EXIT TO BROOKLYN	*Hubert Selby Jr.*	50p
☐	552 09050 6	PASSIONS OF THE MIND	*Irving Stone*	75p
☐	552 07807 7	VALLEY OF THE DOLLS	*Jacqueline Susann*	40p
☐	552 08523 5	THE LOVE MACHINE	*Jacqueline Susann*	40p
☐	552 08384 4	EXODUS	*Leon Uris*	50p
☐	552 08866 6	QB VII	*Leon Uris*	50p
☐	552 08481 6	FOREVER AMBER Vol. 1	*Kathleen Winsor*	40p
☐	552 08482 4	FOREVER AMBER Vol. 2	*Kathleen Winsor*	40p

War

☐	552 09282 7	THE MAN WHO HIT THE SCHARNHORST (illustrated)	*John Austin*	35p
☐	552 09283 5	TO SEA IN A SIEVE	*Peter Bull*	30p
☐	552 09246 0	MAUTHAUSEN: HISTORY OF A DEATH CAMP (illustrated)	*Evelyn le Chêne*	40p
☐	552 08874 9	SS GENERAL	*Sven Hassel*	35p
☐	552 09178 2	REIGN OF HELL	*Sven Hassel*	35p
☐	552 09245 2	BEWARE THE WOUNDED TIGER	*Geoff Taylor*	30p
☐	552 08986 9	DUEL OF EAGLES (illustrated)	*Peter Townsend*	50p
☐	552 09260 6	FINALE AT FLENSBURG (illustrated)	*Charles Whiting*	35p
☐	552 09222 3	BEYOND THE TUMULT (illustrated)	*Barry Winchester*	40p

Romance

☐	552 09288 6	RING O' ROSES	*Lucilla Andrews*	30p
☐	552 09208 8	BRIDAL ARRAY	*Elizabeth Cadell*	30p
☐	552 09209 6	SPRING GREEN	*Elizabeth Cadell*	30p
☐	552 09228 2	THE SEVEN SLEEPERS	*Kate Norway*	30p
☐	552 09248 7	THE FARTHER OFF FROM ENGLAND	*Jean Ure*	30p

Science Fiction

☐	552 09237 1	FANTASTIC VOYAGE	*Isaac Asimov*	35p
☐	552 09289 4	STAR TREK 8	*James Blish*	30p
☐	552 09333 5	THE GOLDEN APPLES OF THE SUN	*Ray Bradbury*	35p
☐	552 09236 3	DRAGONFLIGHT	*Ann McCaffrey*	35p
☐	552 09239 8	MORE THAN HUMAN	*Theodore Sturgeon*	35p

General

☐ 552 09292 4	LOVE, LIFE AND SEX	*Barbara Cartland*	35p
☐ 552 09151 0	THE DRAGON AND THE PHOENIX	*Eric Chou*	50p
☐ 552 98958 4	THE ISLAND RACE Vol. 1	*Winston S. Churchill*	125p
☐ 552 98959 5	THE ISLAND RACE Vol. 2	*Winston S. Churchill*	125p
☐ 552 08800 5	CHARIOTS OF THE GODS? (illustrated)	*Erich von Daniken*	35p
☐ 552 09073 2	RETURN TO THE STARS (illustrated)	*Erich von Daniken*	40p
☐ 552 07400 4	MY LIFE AND LOVES	*Frank Harris*	65p
☐ 552 98748 4	MAKING LOVE (Photographs)	*Walter Hartford*	85p
☐ 552 09135 9	THE HUMAN ANIMAL (illustrated)	*Hans Hass*	40p
☐ 552 09062 X	THE SENSUOUS MAN	*'M'*	35p
☐ 552 09116 2	A BRITISH SURVEY IN FEMALE SEXUALITY	*Sandra McDermott*	40p
☐ 552 08069 1	THE OTHER VICTORIANS	*Steven Marcus*	50p
☐ 552 09291 6	THE ROAD PAST MANDALAY	*John Masters*	40p
☐ 552 08010 1	THE NAKED APE	*Desmond Morris*	30p
☐ 552 09290 8	INTIMATE BEHAVIOUR	*Desmond Morris*	40p
☐ 552 09293 2	GOLF'S WINNING STROKE: PUTTING (illustrated	*Tom Michael*	50p
☐ 552 09232 0	SECRET OF THE ANDES	*Brother Philip*	30p
☐ 552 08880 3	THE THIRTEENTH CANDLE	*T. Lobsang Rampa*	25p
☐ 552 09266 5	ANY WOMAN CAN	*David R. Reuben M.D.*	50p
☐ 552 09044 1	SEX ENERGY	*Robert S. de Ropp*	35p
☐ 552 09250 9	THE MANIPULATED MAN	*Esther Vilar*	35p
☐ 552 09145 6	THE NYMPHO AND OTHER MANIACS	*Irving Wallace*	40p

Western

☐ 552 09147 2	IN THE DAYS OF VICTORIO (illustrated)	*Eve Ball*	40p
☐ 552 07976 6	SUDDEN AT BAY	*Frederick H. Christian*	25p
☐ 552 09095 6	APACHE	*Will Levington Comfort*	30p
☐ 552 09113 8	TWO MILES TO THE BORDER No. 70	*J. T. Edson*	25p
☐ 552 09227 4	YOU'RE IN COMMAND NOW, MR. FOG No. 71	*J. T. Edson*	30p
☐ 552 09298 3	THE BIG GUN No. 72	*J. T. Edson*	30p
☐ 552 09191 X	TREASURE MOUNTAIN	*Louis L'Amour*	30p
☐ 552 09264 9	THE FERGUSON RIFLE	*Louis L'Amour*	30p
☐ 552 09247 9	RANSOM No. 20	*Louis Masterson*	25p
☐ 552 09287 8	KILLING FOR THE LAW No. 21	*Louis Masterson*	25p
☐ 552 09097 2	VALLEY OF THE SHADOW	*Charles Marquis Warren*	35p

Crime

☐ 552 09296 7	LET'S KILL UNCLE LIONEL	*John Creasey*	30p
☐ 552 09297 5	CALL FOR THE BARON	*John Creasey*	30p
☐ 552 09286 X	MURDER MOST FOUL	*John Creasey*	30p
☐ 552 09205 3	THE EXECUTIONER: ASSAULT ON SOHO		30p
☐ 552 09206 1	THE EXECUTIONER: NIGHTMARE IN NEW YORK		30p
☐ 552 09262 2	THE EXECUTIONER: CHICAGO WIPEOUT	*Don Pendleton*	30p
☐ 552 09111 1	THE ERECTION SET	*Mickey Spillane*	40p
☐ 552 09056 5	SHAFT	*Ernest Tidyman*	30p
☐ 552 09072 7	SHAFT'S BIG SCORE	*Ernest Tidyman*	30p
☐ 552 09273 8	SHAFT HAS A BALL	*Ernest Tidyman*	30p

All these books are available at your bookshop or newsagent; or can be ordered direct from the publisher. Just tick the titles you want and fill in the form below.

CORGI BOOKS, Cash Sales Department, P.O. Box 11, Falmouth, Cornwall.

Please send cheque or postal order. No currency, and allow 7p per book to cover the cost of postage and packing in the U.K. (5p if more than one copy), 7p per book overseas.

NAME..

ADDRESS ....

(AUGUST 73) ....